Death and a Pep

A Pumpkin Ho.

By

Kathleen Suzette

Books by Kathleen Suzette:

A Rainey Daye Cozy Mystery Series

Clam Chowder and a Murder
A Rainey Daye Cozy Mystery, book 1
A Short Stack and a Murder
A Rainey Daye Cozy Mystery, book 2
Cherry Pie and a Murder
A Rainey Daye Cozy Mystery, book 3
Barbecue and a Murder
A Rainey Daye Cozy Mystery, book 4
Birthday Cake and a Murder
A Rainey Daye Cozy Mystery, book 5
Hot Cider and a Murder
A Rainey Daye Cozy Mystery, book 6
Roast Turkey and a Murder
A Rainey Daye Cozy Mystery, book 7
Gingerbread and a Murder
A Rainey Daye Cozy Mystery, book 8
Fish Fry and a Murder
A Rainey Daye Cozy Mystery, book 9
Cupcakes and a Murder
A Rainey Daye Cozy Mystery, book 10
Lemon Pie and a Murder
A Rainey Daye Cozy Mystery, book 11
Pasta and a Murder
A Rainey Daye Cozy Mystery, book 12
Chocolate Cake and a Murder
A Rainey Daye Cozy Mystery, book 13

Chocolate Heart Killer
A Pumpkin Hollow Mystery, book 14
Strawberry Creams and Death
A Pumpkin Hollow Mystery, book 15
Pumpkin Spice Lies
A Pumpkin Hollow Mystery, book 16
Sweetly Dead
A Pumpkin Hollow Mystery, book 17
Deadly Valentine
A Pumpkin Hollow Mystery, book 18
Death and a Peppermint Patty
A Pumpkin Hollow Mystery, book 19

A Freshly Baked Cozy Mystery Series

Apple Pie a la Murder,
A Freshly Baked Cozy Mystery, Book 1
Trick or Treat and Murder,
A Freshly Baked Cozy Mystery, Book 2
Thankfully Dead
A Freshly Baked Cozy Mystery, Book 3
Candy Cane Killer
A Freshly Baked Cozy Mystery, Book 4
Ice Cold Murder
A Freshly Baked Cozy Mystery, Book 5
Love is Murder
A Freshly Baked Cozy Mystery, Book 6
Strawberry Surprise Killer
A Freshly Baked Cozy Mystery, Book 7
Plum Dead
A Freshly Baked Cozy Mystery, book 8

Red, White, and Blue Murder
A Freshly Baked Cozy Mystery, book 9
Mummy Pie Murder
A Freshly Baked Cozy Mystery, book 10
Wedding Bell Blunders
A Freshly Baked Cozy Mystery, book 11

A Lemon Creek Mystery Series

Murder at the Ranch
A Lemon Creek Mystery, book 1

A Gracie Williams Mystery Series

Pushing Up Daisies in Arizona,
A Gracie Williams Mystery, Book 1
Kicked the Bucket in Arizona,
A Gracie Williams Mystery, Book 2

A Home Economics Mystery Series

Appliqued to Death
A Home Economics Mystery, book 1

Chapter One

"ARE YOU EXCITED?" ETHAN asked me.

I nodded. "I'm so excited. I don't have to cook dinner tonight. What more could I ask for?"

He chuckled as he pulled into the parking lot of Murphy's Pub. The parking lot was nearly full, and the grand opening sign above the door swayed in the breeze. "I heard they have great food here."

I nodded. "I heard the same thing. I hope Christy and Devon were able to get a table." My sister Christy and her boyfriend Devon had gone on ahead of us, but from the looks of the parking lot, I wasn't sure they would be able to find a place to sit.

Murphy's Pub had opened a week earlier, three weeks before St. Patrick's Day. It promised an authentic Irish Pub experience, or at least as authentic as you were going to get around here. Fortunately, they sold food as well as alcohol. I didn't care about drinking much, but if the food was as good as everyone said it was, then I knew I wouldn't regret the trip.

We got out of the truck and headed to the front door. The snow that had plagued us last month was finally melting, and spring promised to be just around the corner. I hoped I wouldn't be disappointed.

Ethan pushed the door open, and I followed him inside. We stopped and looked around, and I was surprised that the pub was well lit. I guess I had had it in my head that this was going to be some dark, seedy bar, but it wasn't. There were shamrock cutouts along the wall, and standing behind the bar was a big leprechaun. Or rather, a man dressed as a leprechaun. He had gone all out and colored his face green, and he was wearing a green suit and a green top hat. I could hear him talking to one of the customers from where I stood, and he had what sounded like an authentic Irish brogue.

I looked at Ethan. "Who did you say opened this place?"

He turned to me. "I heard it was Jake and Sabrina Hall."

"The leprechaun's accent sounds authentic," I said over the din of the crowd. It looked like half of Pumpkin Hollow had shown up tonight.

He nodded, and a hostess approached us. "Hello, welcome to Murphy's. Would you like a table? Or did you want to sit at the bar? The booths are all filled, or I'd offer you one of those."

"We're meeting my sister and her boyfriend here," I told her, glancing around the room. "And I think I see them over there." I pointed to a corner booth where Christy and Devon were sitting.

She glanced in the direction I pointed. "Why don't you go on over, and someone will be by to take your drink order in a minute."

I nodded, and we weaved our way through the crowd.

"Hey guys," I said when we got to their table. "How are you doing tonight?"

"We're great," Devon said. "How are you two doing?"

"We're happy to get out of the house," Ethan said.

We slid into the booth across from them.

"How's the food?" I asked. Christy had mentioned wanting to come for dinner the night before, and she didn't work today, so I hadn't had a chance to ask how she liked it.

Devon shrugged. "This is our first time here, so we're all going to find out together."

"We tried to stop by last night, but the place was packed, and we decided on pizza instead. It's a good thing we got here early tonight, or we wouldn't have gotten this booth."

"Looks like it's a popular place," Ethan said, looking around at the crowd.

Christy nodded. "Look, Mia, green peanuts." She pushed the bowl over to me. The peanut shells were dyed green.

"Will you look at that," I said. "I don't believe I've ever seen green peanuts before."

Ethan reached into the bowl and picked out two peanuts, cracked the shells, and popped them into his mouth. He nodded as he chewed. "They taste just like regular peanuts. I was hoping they would be lime flavored."

I looked at him, one eyebrow raised. "Lime flavored? It's peppermint patty season, you know."

He shrugged. "I'll take either. But it's just a regular peanut."

I picked up a menu and took a look at it. "They've got a lot of burgers here," I said.

Christy took a sip from her glass of water. "I heard the food is good."

"Don't you want the haggis?" Devon asked.

I looked at him and shook my head. "No. I've heard about what they put in haggis, and there's no chance of me ever touching that. I'm surprised they've got it on the menu."

Devon shook his head. "Come on, Mia, live a little."

"You live a little, Devon. I'm going to stick with something nice and safe like a burger."

Ethan chuckled. "The Ortega burger looks good."

"That's more like it," I said. "Oh, but they've got a teriyaki burger too, and I like that."

"Ethan, you've got to have a green beer," Devon said, holding up his beer mug. It was the biggest beer mug I'd ever seen, and the beer was as green as could be.

He nodded. "I'm not going to pass up the green beer."

The barmaid was Marissa Fields, a young woman I had known for several years. She took our drink orders. Ethan did order his green beer, but I settled on a Coke.

"I hope my Coke isn't going to be green," I said.

Christy chuckled. "It would be hard to dye a Coke green. It's too dark."

The barmaid brought our drinks by, and then a waitress came and took our orders. I settled on the teriyaki burger, and Ethan got the Ortega burger. Christy ordered a pepper jack cheeseburger, and Devon ordered a bacon cheeseburger. The haggis remained on the menu where it belonged.

"How are the candy sales going?" Devon asked, sitting back in his seat. "Is St. Patrick's Day a big candy buying holiday?"

"Not ordinarily," I said. "At least not compared to Valentine's Day. But our mother has been experimenting with lots of mint and peppermint-flavored candy. She's got a mint chocolate chip fudge she's been making for the past two weeks or so."

Christy nodded. "It's pretty tasty. She's also made peppermint patties, and they're good too."

"How did mint become the patron flavor of St. Patrick's Day?" Ethan asked, looking at me.

I thought about it a moment. "I have no idea. I guess because of all the green shamrocks in Ireland and the fact that mint is green." I shrugged. "That's a good question. But it could also have something to do with McDonald's shamrock shakes."

He laughed and took a sip of his beer. "I'd hate to think that McDonald's has that much sway over a holiday."

"I'm good with chocolate and peppermint," Devon said. "It's one of my favorite flavor combinations."

"You won't hear me complaining," Christy agreed. "We've been selling quite a bit of the St. Patrick's Day candy online, too."

"After Easter is over, we'll get a break with the candy making. Things should slow down some. And that will be a good time to take a vacation," I said to Ethan. "I don't suppose you could get away from work for a few days? Or a week?"

He nodded. "I'll ask for some vacation time. Even if we just took a weekend away, it would be nice."

"I would love to go to the beach." It seemed like it had been forever since I had gone someplace on vacation, not counting our honeymoon last October. With all the snow we'd gotten this winter, I was ready for warmer weather.

"It's a little cold for the beach," he said.

"Maybe so, but it will be warmer there than it is here." I picked out a peanut from the bowl and cracked it open.

He took a drink of his green beer and grimaced. "This is different from what I'm used to."

"It's genuine Irish beer," Devon said. "Or at least that's what the leprechaun behind the bar said."

Ethan looked over at him and chuckled. "Is he really from Ireland?"

"His accent sounds genuine," Devon said. "But I didn't ask him."

I looked around the pub. Nearly every table was filled, and if the food was as good as I'd heard, they would do a lot of business here in Pumpkin Hollow.

Christy glanced around the pub. "This place is hopping tonight."

Ethan nodded. "It's kind of nice. I like it."

There were large-screen televisions to watch sports on, and currently, there was a soccer game on the larger TV.

"I'm starving," Christy said and grabbed a handful of the peanuts and cracked one open.

I nodded. "I'm hungry too. With this many customers, I wonder if we'll have a long wait to get our food."

Christy shook her head. "I hope not. That leprechaun might have to get in the kitchen and help the cook because I could eat a horse tonight."

I chuckled. "Me too." It seemed like lunch had been ages ago, and I wished I'd thought to have a light snack before we left the house. With all these people in here, it might be a while before we were served.

"Devon, how are things going with you?" Ethan asked, sitting back and putting his arm along the back of the booth bench behind me.

"It's going all right. We need to get together and do some snowboarding before the snow's all gone." He took a chug of his beer.

"I've been thinking the same thing. Maybe the girls can pack us a lunch, and we'll go next weekend."

"And we can go shopping while they're snowboarding, Mia," Christy said.

I nodded and took a sip of my Coke. "That sounds like a great plan. I could use some new spring clothes."

The food came, and I was glad that it didn't take them long to bring it to us. My burger was huge and served on an oversized bun, and the fries were wedge cut and crispy the way I like them. I took a bite of my burger, and I was pleased to find that it was juicy and perfectly cooked. I looked at Ethan, and he had his mouth full of food. He nodded at me. When he had swallowed, he said, "This is an excellent burger."

"You can say that again," Christy agreed as she took an oversized bite of her burger.

"I knew this was a great idea," Devon said. "Aren't you glad I thought of it?"

Christy chuckled. "I thought of it."

We dug into our meals, and I found that I could only eat half of my burger and part of my fries. The meal was impressive, and I thought this place might become a regular hangout for us. Pumpkin Hollow had needed another place to get good food.

When we finished, I sat back, my stomach overly full, and groaned. "That was great. We need to come here again next weekend."

"You're telling tell me," Ethan said, looking at his empty plate. "I can't believe I ate the whole thing."

"I can," Devon said. "That's the best burger I've had in a while."

We sat at the table, allowing our meals to digest and talking. I enjoyed having time with some of my favorite people, and I really hoped we would do this often.

The scream that came from the kitchen startled us.

Chapter Two

THE SCREAMS PUT ETHAN on the run. He pulled out his gun as he headed toward the kitchen. Christy and I were on our feet and we ran after him. I know, it could have been a dangerous situation, but we didn't stop to think about it. The staff in the kitchen had stopped what they were doing and were looking at the open back door, frozen in place.

One of the waitresses was standing near the open back door, her face pale. "It's Bubba. Bubba's dead!"

Ethan ran out onto the back step and stopped, glancing around the alley, his gun raised. He must've heard footsteps behind him as Christy and I hurried to catch up to him, because he turned and looked at me, frowning. "Don't come out here!"

Christy and I stopped and watched as he ran out into the night.

The waitress burst out into tears. "Bubba's dead! I can't believe this!"

I glanced around at the workers in the kitchen. There were two cooks, a dishwasher, and four other kitchen staff, as well as two more waitresses.

"What happened? Who's Bubba?" I asked.

The waitress shook her head, her eyes wide. "Somebody killed Bubba. There's blood everywhere out there."

Devon was slower to get out of his seat, and he brought up the rear, coming to a stop behind Christy.

"What's going on?" Devon asked breathlessly.

The waitress looked at him and shook her head again. "Bubba's dead. Somebody killed him." She sniffled and pulled a tissue out of her apron pocket.

"Who's Bubba?" I asked again, my eyes going to the still open back door. Cold air came in through it, but I couldn't see Ethan from where I stood.

"Bubba. The leprechaun." She blew her nose into the tissue.

Bubba the leprechaun?

"The leprechaun?" Christy asked. "Are you kidding me?"

She shook her head. "I'm not kidding you. Somebody killed him. They cut his throat."

I glanced at Christy.

"So much for leprechauns being good luck," she said.

Devon shook his head. "You would think about something like that."

She shrugged. "I'm just saying. Leprechauns are supposed to be good luck, and clearly, if this one is dead, he didn't have much luck."

"I guess his luck ran out," I said. We weren't trying to make light of the situation. I guess you could chalk it up to the shock of someone dying suddenly. I tiptoed over to the back door. Ethan was on the other side of the alley, peering around the side of the dumpster.

He turned to me and shook his head. "I don't see anybody out here."

I nodded and stepped out onto the back step, looking down at the leprechaun. The smell of smoke hung in the air. He was lying on his back, staring up at the sky. Blood covered his neck and the front of his green coat. I shook my head. "Looks like his luck just ran out."

Ethan walked further down the alley, and when he was satisfied that the killer wasn't lurking in the shadows, he turned and came back. "You shouldn't have followed me out here," he said as he came to stand next to the leprechaun. "It's dangerous out here."

I nodded, still staring at the leprechaun. He looked like he was in his early forties, and he made a horrifying picture with his green face and the red blood around his neck. "The waitress said he was stabbed."

Ethan kneeled beside him and looked over the wound on his neck. "Looks more like somebody slashed his throat." He pulled his phone from his pocket and made a call to the police station. He stuck his phone back into his pocket. "Poor guy."

I nodded, crossing my arms in front of me. "Did anyone see anything?" I asked, looking back toward the kitchen.

"You know about as much as I do," he said as he looked over the leprechaun. Christy and Devon stepped out onto the back step.

"Whoa," Devon said when he saw the leprechaun. "His luck really did run out."

"I guess leprechauns aren't as lucky as people make them out to be," Christy said, shaking her head. "Poor sap."

Ethan looked up at us. "Can we quit with the bad luck jokes?"

"We aren't joking," I said. "Honestly, we're sorry that he's dead." I looked at Christy and Devon, and they both nodded.

"Yeah, it's a shame," Christy said, taking a step forward. "What do you think happened?"

Ethan looked up at her. "I think somebody slashed his throat."

She nodded. "Okay, that's the obvious, isn't it? I'm talking about who did it. Mia, let's get looking for clues."

Ethan narrowed his eyes at her and held a hand up. "You two stop right where you are. Neither of you has any business looking for anything. In fact, you shouldn't even be out here. Why don't you go back inside?"

I glanced at Christy and elbowed her. "We aren't going to get in the way. I promise." But my eyes were already searching the ground. There was a light at the back of the building that gave off a fluorescent glare that wasn't very strong. If you stood right at the back door, you got the majority of the light, but just a few feet further than that, and you would be in almost complete darkness.

"Shouldn't you look around the alley?" Christy asked. "The killer might have dropped something."

I elbowed her again. "She knows that you're looking, Ethan."

He shook his head and muttered something I couldn't make out. "Why don't you all go back inside?"

The waitress and the dishwasher stepped out onto the step behind us. They looked past us. "Oh, my gosh," the waitress said breathlessly. "I just can't believe it. It's awful. I can't imagine who would do something like that."

"What was the leprechaun doing back here?" I asked her.

She looked away from the leprechaun. "He was taking a smoke break. He always comes out here to smoke."

That would explain the smell of smoke in the air. "How long has he been out here?" I asked. "Do you know?"

I glanced at Ethan, and he was still examining the victim.

"Oh," she shrugged. "I don't know. Five minutes? Ten? It's been so busy tonight, and I've been running back and forth to and from the kitchen. I didn't notice when he came out here, so I couldn't say how long it's been."

"I think it's been closer to twenty minutes," the dishwasher said, his eyes on the dead leprechaun. "I saw him come out here a while ago, and I swear it had to be at least twenty minutes ago."

I couldn't remember when the last time was that I had seen the leprechaun inside the pub. "Twenty minutes is a long time for a smoke break."

He nodded. "Yeah, but the only thing that leprechaun had to do was greet people and hang out at the bar. It's not like anybody was going to miss him if he took extra time on a break."

My eyes went to the dishwasher. He sounded almost bitter when he said it.

Ethan looked up at him. "I don't want anybody leaving the premises. Have any of the customers had any access to this door?" he asked.

The waitress shook her head. "No, the only way you can get to this landing is through this back door, and you have to go through the kitchen. Do you want me to hold all the customers?"

He thought about it for a moment, and then he shook his head. "No, if nobody's had access back here, then I'm not going to worry about them. But all the employees need to stay put. Can you let them know that?"

She nodded and went back into the kitchen.

We heard sirens in the distance, and within a few minutes, a police car pulled into the alley. Ethan looked up at the car and got to his feet. He headed over to the squad car when it had parked.

Christy turned and looked at me, one eyebrow raised. "I wonder what happened? Who would kill a leprechaun?"

"It seems almost cruel," I said. "Leprechauns are supposed to be happy."

"Well, he's not happy anymore," Devon said, shoving his hands into his pockets.

I snorted and shook my head. "That's for sure." I glanced at Ethan. "We better keep our remarks to herself, or we're going to make Ethan angry."

Christy nodded. "I wonder if he found the pot of gold at the end of the rainbow?"

I eyed her. "Didn't I just say that we need to quit saying things like that?"

She shrugged. "Ethan can't hear me, and I had to say it. It was just too good not to. I'll be good now."

"You had better be," I said.

"Maybe Leprechauns are supposed to be happy, but Bubba wasn't the most cheerful person around." We turned and looked at the dishwasher.

"Why do you say that?" I asked.

He shook his head. "The guy was a jerk. And he's not really Irish, either. That accent was fake."

"It sounded pretty authentic to me," I said, glancing back at the leprechaun.

"Yeah, well, he's probably never even been to Ireland. It was all fake. That's how he got the job. Because he was the owner's cousin and because he could fake an Irish accent well enough to fool the customers."

The dishwasher sounded bitter when he spoke about Bubba, and it made me wonder.

Ethan and the other officer headed back over to the leprechaun, and Ethan looked up at us. "I thought you three were going to go inside? Can you wait inside for me?"

I nodded. "Christy and Devon, let's go inside."

It was a shame that the leprechaun had died. The pub was new in town, and it looked like it was going to do a good business. Would a murder put a damper on things?

Chapter Three

"I AM STARVING," CHRISTY said as she bent over and sniffed the closed box of donuts in her hands.

"Me too," I said as we got out of my car and headed into the candy store. We had stopped off at the bakery and picked up a dozen donuts and peppermint mochas for everyone at the candy store. St. Patrick's Day may not have been a huge candy buying season, but that didn't stop us from creating lots of peppermint flavored candy for the holiday. The online and store sales had been brisk, despite the lack of a traditional candy buying holiday. Because, who doesn't like peppermint?

"We're here!" Christy called as we walked through the candy store and headed toward the kitchen with the donuts and coffee.

"Did you bring donuts?" Carrie Green asked from the corner of the store where she was dusting shelves.

"And coffee," I said, glancing over my shoulder at her.

"You two are my favorite people," she said and followed us back to the kitchen. "I love donuts."

"Me too," Christy said. "I love donuts almost as much as I love fudge."

My mother and Linda Reid were in the kitchen making candy. The scent of peppermint and chocolate hung in the air. "I hope you all are hungry for donuts," I said.

They turned to look at us. "Oh, my goodness, you girls knew exactly what I needed this morning," Mom said. "I was thinking about donuts as I was making the fudge."

You would think that by working in a candy store that we all had had more than our fair share of sugar, but the donuts from the Sweet Goblin bakery were delectable, and who doesn't like donuts?

"We picked up peppermint mochas too," I said, setting the cardboard drink carrier on the counter. Christy set the box of donuts next to them and opened the lid and inhaled.

"Look at these shamrock-shaped donuts," Christy said. "Angela outdid herself."

The Shamrock-shaped donuts were similar to a Boston cream, with chocolate icing and peppermint cream filling. She had somehow made them in the shape of a Shamrock, and I just had to have one. I grabbed a napkin and picked one out of the box, and took a bite. I groaned. I held my thumb and finger up, making an 'O', and nodded. "This is an excellent donut. You all had better get one of these, or I'm going to eat them all myself."

"They look tasty," Linda said as she picked up a donut and took a bite. She nodded. "Excellent. Angela has a gift for baked goods."

"Save some for me," Carrie said, reaching for a coffee.

I turned to her. "You had better get a donut, or there won't be any left."

"Thank you so much for bringing these." She picked up a green sprinkle donut. "I love the donuts from the Sweet Goblin bakery."

"You and me both," I said as I took another bite of my donut. It was delicious.

Carrie took a sip of her coffee and turned to me. "So I heard there was some excitement at the new pub last night?"

I nodded, glancing at Christy. Ethan had sent us home after ordering us back inside the pub several times. I didn't mean to annoy him, but everybody was in shock over the murder, so we had hung out on the back step as long as he would allow it. Christy and Devon had dropped me off at home, and it was late by the time he got home. He had mumbled a hello and fallen asleep. He was up and out of bed early this morning, and I hadn't gotten to talk to him much about the case yet.

"Somebody killed a leprechaun," Christy said. "His luck ran out."

Linda chuckled. "You're terrible, Christy."

I glanced at Christy and shook my head. "That poor leprechaun can't catch a break."

"Who was the leprechaun?" Mom asked. "Do we know him?"

I shook my head. "His name was Bubba, but I don't know what his last name is. Ethan got in so late that we didn't have time to talk about it much."

"Jake and Sabrina Hall opened up that new pub," Linda said. "I hear the food is really good. Is it?"

I nodded. "They serve excellent food."

Christy selected a cake donut covered in green icing from the box. "They're going to do a great business. At least, as long as this murder doesn't hurt them. But the food is great."

"Jake and Sabrina opened it?" I asked and took a sip of my coffee.

Linda nodded. "Yes, although I think it was more his idea than hers. But Pumpkin Hollow can always do with another restaurant."

I nodded. "It's actually pretty nice inside. I was afraid it would be more like a bar than a restaurant, but I think they achieved a nice balance of restaurant and bar."

"I'll have to have my husband take me one night," Linda said and took a sip of her coffee. "How did the leprechaun die?"

Christy turned to her. "There was no pot of gold at the end of the rainbow, and he died of disappointment. Bad luck for him."

I shook my head at Linda. "Ignore her. She can't get past the bad luck jokes. Somebody slashed his throat."

Linda gasped. "Oh, my gosh. How awful. Right there in the pub?"

I finished my donut and looked at the rest of the donuts in the box. The last thing I needed was another donut. "No, he was out back taking a smoke break."

"Didn't Jake Hall used to sell life insurance?" Mom asked as she went to the refrigerator.

"I don't know," I said. Jake came into the candy store occasionally and liked chocolate fudge without nuts. "I never thought to ask where he worked."

I didn't know either Jake or Sabrina well, but they were regular customers of ours.

She nodded and took some butter out of the refrigerator, and brought it over to the counter. "If I'm thinking right, that's what he used to do. I wonder what made him open up a pub?"

"Maybe it was a dream of his," Linda said. "I wouldn't think selling insurance would be a lot of fun. Opening a pub might be fun, though."

"You know," Carrie said thoughtfully. "If I'm not mistaken, I think the Halls had some financial issues. I guess that's probably gossip, but it surprises me that they turned around and opened up a pub. I would imagine that cost an awful lot of money."

I hesitated. "Money problems? What do you mean?"

She shrugged. "Their house was in foreclosure."

I looked at her. This was mildly interesting. How did one go from having a house in foreclosure to owning a pub?

"I wonder where they got the money for the pub then?" Christy asked. "That old building they set it up in had to be completely remodeled to be turned into a pub."

Christy had a point. There had been a clothing store in that building several years earlier, so it would have taken a complete remodel. If a restaurant or bar had been there previously, it wouldn't have needed quite as much work, but as it was, they would have had to put everything brand-new in there.

Carrie shrugged. "Maybe things turned around for them."

"How do you know about the foreclosure?" I asked.

"There was a for sale sign on their house several months ago. When Sabrina came into the candy store, I asked her if they were planning on moving away, and she shrugged and said the house was in foreclosure and they were hoping to sell it before the bank took it back."

I decided that I had to have another donut, and I picked one with green sprinkles. "So maybe they did sell it? Maybe they got more money than what they owed, and that helped to open up the pub."

She nodded. "That's possible. And I bet that's what happened. They probably made some extra money on the sale of the house, and they used it to open the pub," Carrie said.

"That sounds like the most logical explanation," Christy said, glancing at me. The glance told me that Christy wasn't completely convinced that this was what happened. But until we knew something more definite, it was just as likely as anything else.

"What are you making today, Mom?" I asked.

She turned to me. "Mint chocolate chip fudge. It's selling like hotcakes." She chuckled. "Or maybe it's selling like mint chocolate chip fudge. Whatever."

I grinned. "I love your mint chocolate chip fudge." Mom tinted the fudge with green food coloring, and it had been a hit with everyone looking for a treat for St. Patty's day.

"I love your peppermint patties," Christy said. "Are you going to make some more of those?"

She nodded. "I sure am. Those are selling like hotcakes, too." She went to the refrigerator and got some heavy cream out and set it on the counter.

I finished my donut and took a sip of my coffee before getting to work. I didn't know what had happened to the leprechaun yet, but I knew that Christy and I would certainly try to figure out who killed him.

Chapter Four

"WHAT DO YOU THINK?" Christy asked me as we sat in my car outside of Jake and Sabrina Hall's house.

I glanced up at it. It was a two-story modern stucco. The development was a recent one, having only begun a year before. From what I'd heard, the houses were pricey. Opening up a pub on top of buying a brand-new house would be expensive, especially if their other house had gone into foreclosure. But maybe things had turned around for the Halls, and they didn't have any trouble financing both.

I shook my head and looked at her. "Looks like a nice house. I'd love to be able to buy a house over here."

She turned and looked at the house again and nodded. "You and me both. I bet these houses will set you back a pretty penny."

I opened my car door and got out while she got out on her side. "That's what I heard. But a girl can dream."

We headed up the sidewalk, and I knocked on the door. For it still being mid-March, we'd had a few days of warm weather, and what snow was left from the last storm was quickly melting away. I hoped we'd seen the last of the snow for the season, but I wouldn't be surprised if we had a few more days of it left.

Sabrina opened the door, and she looked surprised to see us. "Oh. Hello Mia, hello Christy." She looked from me to Christy and smiled.

"Good morning, Sabrina," I said. "We were at the pub the other night when Bubba was killed, and we thought we'd stop by and tell you how sorry we were about it."

She frowned, nodding. "Yes, Bubba was my husband's cousin. He's broken up about it."

"I'm so sorry about his death." Christy held up a tin of fudge. "We brought you some fudge. Our mom insisted."

Her eyes went to the tin, and she smiled. "That's so sweet of her. You tell her I appreciate that, and I appreciate you two stopping by. Would you like to come in?"

"Sure, we've got a few minutes before we have to be at work," I said.

We followed her into the house and I was just as impressed with the inside as I was the outside. The wooden floors gleamed, and everything was so new and bright. "You have a lovely home."

She looked over her shoulder and smiled. "Thank you so much. Jake and I have talked about buying a new house for years, and when this new development started up, I told him how much I wanted to buy one of these homes." She motioned to the couch, and we took a seat as she sat across from us.

"I'm envious," Christy said as she glanced around the house. Sabrina went for stylishly modern furnishings, and as we sat down, we sank into the leather sofa.

I sighed. "Oh my gosh, this is the most comfortable couch I've ever sat on." The couch was so comfortable you could have taken a nap on it. Someday I wanted to buy a couch like this.

She beamed. "It's the first new furniture I've ever owned in my life. I've always had hand-me-downs, but I told Jake that if we were moving into a brand-new house, then I wanted brand-new furniture."

"All I've ever had was hand-me-downs, too," Christy said, eyeing me. She had inherited Ethan's furniture after we got married when she moved into the little cottage across the street that he had occupied. It was just easy to leave all of his furniture there since I had my own, and she didn't have much, anyway.

Sabrina chuckled. "Well, we saved up all our lives to be able to buy this house. I told my husband that I was going to have exactly what I wanted, so that's what we got."

I nodded, wondering about the foreclosure. "It certainly is lovely."

"You used to live on Spooky Springs Avenue, didn't you?" Christy asked.

She hesitated. "Yes, we did. That house went into foreclosure, and I told Jake we had better try to sell it before the bank takes it back. We found an investor that was more than generous with his offer, thank goodness."

"What good luck for you," Christy said.

She nodded. "It really was."

"Sabrina, I'm so sorry about Bubba. It was just awful what happened to him," I said.

She sobered and sat back on the loveseat. "It was just awful. Jake feels terrible because we weren't there that night. But you wouldn't believe the hours we put in down there in the months that led up to the grand opening. We've also been there every day and every evening since it first opened. I had insisted that we take the evening off that night. We stayed here all evening and watched TV and ordered a pizza for dinner. It was the first night we had to relax and enjoy ourselves in months. I told him he shouldn't feel bad that we weren't there."

I nodded. "I'm sure it takes an awful lot of work to open up a pub."

She sighed. "You have no idea. Honestly, we didn't know what we were getting ourselves into. Between opening up a new pub and then moving into this new house, it just seems like forever since we've been able to slow down. And the one night we took off, Bubba was murdered." She made a clucking sound and shook her head. "It just seems unthinkable."

"Was Bubba from around here?" I asked her. I was sure he couldn't be a local since I'd never seen him before.

She shook her head. "No, he just moved here from Ohio a few months ago. He lost his job at a factory there, and Jake suggested that he come to work for him here. Now Jake feels so guilty about the whole thing. But I told him there was no way he could have predicted something as terrible as this was going to happen. But he has always taken on responsibility that doesn't belong to him. I told him when I married him that he was the most responsible person I had ever met, and I was right about that."

"Bubba was from Ohio? Had he lived there long?" Christy asked.

She nodded. "Yes, he lived there for over twenty years if I remember right. Why?"

Christy shrugged. "I heard him talking to some customers, and he had an Irish accent. It sounded so authentic."

Sabrina chuckled. "Yes, wasn't he good at that? But no, he was born in New Jersey. Can you believe it? He was born in New Jersey and moved to Ohio and had never seen Ireland, as far as I know."

"He was good at accents then," I said. I would have sworn the leprechaun was Irish after hearing him speak.

She nodded. "Yes, he could do a Texas drawl, a French accent, and the Irish accent. He was hysterical. If you had gotten the chance to get to know him, you would've seen that. He was dead on with his accents, and he was so funny."

"Wow, how great that he could do that and make people think he was from Ireland since you opened the pub," I said.

She nodded. "Yes, Jake had always wanted to open up an Irish pub, and when Bubba lost his job, he knew that he would be perfect. He thought he could come and work for us and entertain the diners and patrons. Not that he would have played a leprechaun all year long, of course, but he would have kept the customers entertained, regardless. He made up all these stories he was going to tell the customers about his life in Ireland."

"He was so convincing," Christy said.

"Do you have any idea what might've happened to him?" I asked her.

She hesitated. "Well, I really don't know. Honestly, I'm shocked that this happened to him. But you know Archie, our dishwasher? The two of them didn't get along very well. I'm not saying that there was anything serious between them, but it seemed like they were always arguing with one another. I mentioned it to Jake, but he just shrugged it off. Honestly, if there was an issue between the two of them, he would have been too busy to realize anything was going on. I tell you, we just ran ourselves ragged these past months." She chuckled.

"But you noticed that there was something between the two of them?" I asked.

She nodded. "Honestly, two days before we opened the pub, both Bubba and Archie got into an argument. I missed the beginning of the argument, so I'm not quite sure what it was about. But I ran into the kitchen to see what was going on when I heard shouting, and the two of them were so angry. They were both red-faced, and I asked what was going on. But neither of them would tell me what had happened."

"Did you hear anything specific?" Christy asked.

She thought about it a moment. "Archie was angry at Bubba. To be honest, Bubba was a little on the lazy side. My husband had the idea for him to be the leprechaun during the first couple of weeks since it was so close to St. Patrick's Day. Later he was going to be a sort of maître d', but his job was always undefined. I honestly just think that Jake wanted to hire him as a favor. He was family, after all, and he did have that Irish accent. He loved to entertain, and he loved to talk to people. And I think Archie was a little resentful about it."

"Why would he be resentful, though? If he was hired for a job, why would he care about what somebody else's job was?" Christy asked.

She shrugged. "To be honest, I really have no idea. I told Jake about the argument, and he brushed it off. He said he would speak to them, but I forgot about it, and I never asked if he did."

"It's a shame that he died," I said.

She sighed. "It hasn't really sunk in that he's gone. I'm not saying that Archie had something to do with his death, though. I don't think he would do something like that."

I nodded. Arguing so angrily made me wonder about him, though. "Well, we've got to get to work. We just wanted to stop in and say hello and tell you how sorry we were for your loss."

She got to her feet. "I appreciate you girls stopping by. And tell your mother thank you for sending the fudge. She makes the best fudge in the world."

We said our goodbyes and headed out the front door.

When the door closed behind us, Christy turned to look at me. "What do you think?"

"I'm wondering about Archie. Even if he thought Bubba was lazy, he was hired for a job as a dishwasher. What business was it of his what Bubba was doing?"

She nodded, and we got into my car. "And besides that, he was related to the owner. It's not like he was going to do anything about Bubba being lazy. That's a lost cause."

Christy had a point. Sometimes when you worked in a family business, things like that happened. Not that we had a problem with that at the candy store, but I could see it happening elsewhere.

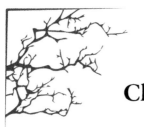

Chapter Five

"WHERE'S THE BABY?" I asked Amanda.

She looked at me, her brow furrowed. "What? No hello, Amanda? No, how are you doing, Amanda?"

I chuckled. "Hello, Amanda. How are you doing, Amanda?"

She grinned. "I'm doing great, Mia. Thank you for asking."

I stepped up to the front counter of the Little Coffee Shop of Horrors. My friend Amanda and her husband Brian owned it, and they served the best coffee and scones in town.

"And how is that beautiful baby? And where is she?" I couldn't help myself. I was having baby withdrawals.

She smiled and shrugged. "My mother had the day off from work, and she insisted that she keep her today. Sorry, but I'm sure she'll be back tomorrow."

I sighed melodramatically. "All right, fine. I guess her grandmother ranks higher than I do. I'll just have to stop back in tomorrow and give her a squeeze."

Isabella Grace was nine months old, and she was the sweetest baby I've ever seen. Until she got more mobile,

Amanda was bringing her with her to work. I looked up at the menu board. "How about a vanilla mummy latte?"

She nodded. "You got it," she said and got to work on my coffee. "I heard there was some excitement over at the new pub the other night."

I nodded. "Yeah, the leprechaun got killed." I refrained from making any bad luck jokes. Although if I were being truthful, I'd have to admit that there were several of them on the tip of my tongue.

She shook her head. "How awful. Who kills a leprechaun? Don't they know that's bad luck? Think of all the gold at the end of the rainbow that was lost when they did that."

I snorted and shook my head. "Oh gosh, there are so many things I could say about that. It would have been nice if he would have told us where the pot of gold was before he crossed the rainbow bridge." All right, it was bad. I couldn't help myself. But it was her fault since she started it.

She chuckled as she poured vanilla syrup into my drink. "In all seriousness, what happened?"

I shrugged and leaned on the front counter, gazing into the baked goods display case. "Someone slashed his throat when he was taking a smoke break out back. Ethan's on the case, so hopefully, he'll get it straightened out soon."

She shook her head. "That's a shame. Smoking is bad for your health though."

I looked at her, one eyebrow raised. "It's a killer." We turned as the front door opened, and Marissa Fields, one of the barmaids from the pub, walked through the door.

"Hello Mia, hello, Amanda. How are you two doing today?"

I smiled at her. "I'm doing all right. The weather has been lovely these past several days, and I am ready for spring."

She nodded. "How is Ethan doing on Bubba's murder case?" she asked, coming to stand beside me.

I shook my head. "You know how it is. He's hunting a killer, but he doesn't always tell me everything he knows, especially in the beginning." Ethan hadn't told me much of anything yet, but if he had, I wouldn't spread around.

She looked up at the menu board and then glanced back at me again. "I was pretty excited to get a job down there at the pub. I worked over at a restaurant in Truckee, but I got laid off four months ago when it closed before Thanksgiving."

"I bet you were excited about getting a new job then," Amanda said.

She nodded. "I sure was. But I have to say, it's rough down there."

I was all ears now. "Oh? What do you mean?"

She crossed her arms in front of herself. "There are several people that are pretty grumpy down there, and Jake Hall is a hard person to work for."

I was surprised at this. I had thought Jake was fairly easygoing. "What do you mean he's hard to work for?"

Her eyes went to the menu board again, but then she looked back at me. "It's just that he can be kind of short with people. You ask a question, and you don't get much by way of explanation. It just makes things hard."

"Yeah, I guess that would make things hard," I agreed. Starting a new job and not getting much in the way of instruction would be frustrating, to say the least.

She nodded. "Yeah, and with it being a whole new staff where nobody has worked with one another, there can be issues, if you know what I mean."

I wasn't exactly sure that I did know what she meant. "I guess nobody worked with one another previously then?" I would have thought that Jake had hired staff that had worked at the local restaurants and bars, and with Pumpkin Hollow being a small town, I would also have thought at least some of them had worked together at some point.

She shook her head. "No, none of us had worked with one another, and when you've got somebody that's barking orders and isn't very helpful, it just makes things tense, if you want to know the truth," she said, stopping and glancing over her shoulder. We were the only three in the coffee shop. She turned back to me. "I think Jake has a drinking problem."

I tilted my head. I'd never heard this about Jake before. "Oh? Why do you say that?" I glanced at Amanda as she worked on my coffee.

"I've smelled alcohol on his breath more than a couple of times while we got the place ready to open up. I think it's the reason why he's so short with people."

"I had no idea," I said. "He comes into the candy store fairly regularly, and he always seemed like a really nice guy." Had Jake been drinking, and had he and Bubba gotten into an argument, and he killed him? Sabrina had said she and Jake took the night off, though.

Her eyes widened slightly. "Oh, I don't mean to say that he isn't a nice guy. I mean, he's short with everybody, and he's difficult to work with, but I think it's just because he was so stressed out about opening up the pub. That's probably all it was." She looked away now.

I hadn't meant for my comment to make her stop talking. I needed to know everything she knew in case there was something important that might help with the investigation. "Of course, opening a new pub would be stressful," I agreed. "And maybe if somebody has an issue with alcohol, they might be feeling the pressure and drink a little more. How was Jake's relationship with Bubba? Did you happen to notice?"

She hesitated. "Well, they were cousins, you know. And sometimes there was some arguing between the two of them. I don't know. I think everybody was just under a lot of pressure trying to get the pub opened up on time."

"Did you hear what they were arguing about?"

She sighed thoughtfully. "Well, I know at one point they were arguing about a family member. About an uncle, I think it was. It seems that he died recently, and Bubba wasn't left much in the will." She looked at me meaningfully.

"They said that?" I asked.

She nodded slowly. "Yeah, it sounded like Jake got the lion's share of what was in the will. This uncle didn't have any kids, and the money was split between his nieces and nephews."

Now we were getting somewhere. Maybe that was how Jake and Sabrina had the money to buy both a new house and open up the pub. "I'm sure that that would have made things stressful. Families with money problems tend to do that."

She nodded. "You're telling me. My grandmother left my cousin more money than she left me, and I'm still mad about it." She laughed. "No, I'm really not mad about it. My grandmother didn't have much money to leave, and I think my cousin ended up with fifty bucks more than I got. I tease her all the time about being Grandma's favorite."

I chuckled. "So you know for sure that's what they were arguing about? The uncle leaving more money for Jake?" I asked.

She nodded. "Yeah, they were in the kitchen early one morning, and I arrived before most of the other staff. I could hear them arguing with one another. Bubba was really mad that Jake ended up with the money. He said that Jake sweet-talked his way into all that money."

"Wow," I said as Amanda put my coffee on the front counter, and I dug in my pocket for the money to pay for it. "I guess I can see where someone would get mad about that. But it was Bubba that ended up dead, not Jake." Maybe there was an argument that went too far, and Jake killed his cousin. But how had he ended up at the pub when his wife said he was at home with her?

She shrugged. "That's true. I'm sure it had nothing to do with what happened. Please don't tell anybody that I mentioned this to you. I don't want to lose this job."

I shook my head. "Of course not. I won't say a word."

She looked at Amanda, and she nodded. "Your secret is safe with us. I'm sure Ethan will figure out who the killer is soon, and nobody will have to worry about this anymore."

I handed Amanda the money for the coffee, and Marissa told her what she wanted to order.

"Amanda, I'll see you later. Bye, Marissa," I said as I headed for the front door.

"See you later," Amanda called to me as she got to work on Marissa's order.

"I'll talk to you later," Marissa said to me.

So there was money trouble in the Hall family. That was interesting, and I wondered if Ethan knew that yet.

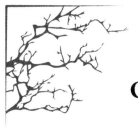

Chapter Six

"YOU ARE A SIGHT FOR sore eyes," Ethan said, pulling me to him and holding me tight.

I chuckled and squeezed him back. "Right back at you." I looked up into his eyes. He looked tired. "How was work?"

He sighed dramatically. "You know how it is. Work is work."

I nodded and took him by the hand and led him inside the house. Our black cats, Boo and Licorice, came running when they heard Ethan's voice.

"Well, two of my very favorite people," he said, kneeling to pet both of them. "I missed you guys."

"They miss you when you're not home," I said to him. "I wonder what they do all day while we're at work?"

He chuckled and shook his head. "I have a feeling that these two don't do a lot more than sleep and eat while we're gone."

"You might be right about that," I said and headed into the kitchen. "How does fried chicken sound?"

He followed me into the kitchen. "You made fried chicken?" he asked, looking at the covered pan on the stove.

I turned and looked at him. "Don't sound so surprised. I'm branching out from the usual pizza and frozen lasagna. Does it make you happy?"

He nodded. "You better believe it. Fried chicken sounds awesome, and it smells really good."

I nodded. "Doesn't it? I might even make some gravy to go along with the mashed potatoes we're having with it."

His eyes got big. "Oh, don't tease me. If you bring up the word gravy you've got to deliver."

I shrugged. "All right, then. I'll make some gravy." I didn't do a lot of cooking, but since we had gotten married, I was doing a little more when I could. There were some days that I was just too tired when I got home from work, and so we probably ate more pizza than we should. But after being on my feet all day, I was usually in no mood to cook.

Licorice and Boo wandered into the kitchen and sat down, looking up at me expectantly. They'd been hovering near the kitchen ever since I took the chicken out of the refrigerator.

"I hope you made some chicken for those two," Ethan said, going to the refrigerator and pulling out the pitcher of iced tea.

"I'm sure they'll get a bite or two of our chicken," I assured him. "So, how was work? Really?"

He shrugged and went to the cupboard and took down two glasses. "Busy. Lots of people to talk to. You know how it is."

Before I could answer, there was a knock at the door, and then it opened. I didn't have to look to know who it was.

"We're in here," I called to my sister.

She closed the door and hurried into the kitchen. "Oh my gosh, don't tell me I just happened to stop by when you were making dinner? How on earth did I manage that?" She inhaled. "Smells good."

I looked at her, one eyebrow raised. "Imagine that. You just happened to show up when I'm making dinner. What a coincidence."

She shrugged dramatically. "Some people just have a gift."

I chuckled. "And I just happened to make some extra food, so if you're hungry, I guess you can hang around."

"Well, I'm not overwhelmed by the invitation. But I think I'll hang out and see what you've got." She went to the stove and lifted the lid on the pan. "Wow. Fried chicken. I haven't had homemade fried chicken in ages."

"Me either," I said as I went to the sink and filled a pot with water for the potatoes. "It just sounded good to me, so that's what we've got."

She turned and looked at Ethan. "Hey Ethan, how's it going?"

He shrugged and took another glass out of the cupboard. "It's going all right. Iced tea?"

She nodded as he filled a glass and handed it to her. "Thanks. You're my favorite brother-in-law, you know."

"I'm honored," he said dryly.

"Ethan, what's going on with the investigation? Have you arrested anyone yet?" she asked, leaning on the kitchen counter.

He shook his head. "Not yet. But soon, I'm sure."

I turned and looked at him. "So, do you have anyone in mind yet?"

He shook his head and took a sip of his iced tea. "Not yet. I don't suppose you two have been snooping around, have you?"

I filled him in on everything we'd found out from Sabrina Hall and Marissa Fields. "It's odd that Marissa brought up Jake's name. Not that it matters, because he was home with his wife all evening."

Ethan had raised his glass halfway to his mouth to take another sip, and he stopped, looking at me. "What?"

I hesitated and took the pot over to the stove and set it on the burner. "Jake and Sabrina were at home that evening. She said they had been working so hard trying to get the pub open that they were exhausted, and they took the night off. Why?" The look in his eyes said something was up.

He took a sip of his iced tea, thinking over what I had just said. "She said they were home the entire evening?"

I nodded, glancing at Christy. "Yes, she said they were home the whole evening. Why?"

"What's going on, Ethan?" Christy asked, taking a step closer. "What do you know?"

He glanced at her, narrowing his eyes. "It's none of your business what I know."

"But you know something," I said, turning the fire on beneath the pot of potatoes.

He was quiet for a moment. "Jake told me he was at the pub earlier in the evening and had left before the murder occurred." He took a sip of his iced tea, deep in thought.

I looked at him sharply. "He said that? How much earlier did he leave?"

He was quiet. "I'll have to look at my notes, but if I remember right, he said it was around six o'clock."

"And we got to the pub at around 6:30," Christy pointed out. "And the leprechaun was killed not long after we got there."

"No, he was killed after we finished eating dinner," I reminded her. "We were sitting at the table talking about how good everything was."

She raised one finger and pointed at me. "You're right. We stayed a few minutes after we finished eating. So let's see, we probably had our food by seven o'clock, and we finished no later than 7:30. Does that sound right?"

"It was 7:45 when we heard the scream," Ethan said.

Christy whistled. "So Jake left around six o'clock. That leaves a lot of time to come back and kill someone. It seems like his wife would have noticed if he had left the house, don't you think?"

He nodded. "I'm sure she would have."

I put the lid on the pot of potatoes. "Unless he had an errand to run. Maybe they wanted something for dessert, and he ran to the grocery store. She said they ordered a pizza for dinner, and if they didn't want to cook dinner, then they probably wouldn't want to make something for dessert."

"I think you need to have another talk with Jake," Christy told him and took a sip of her iced tea. "What if he doubled back and killed the leprechaun while he was on his smoke break?"

"I bet he would have known when Bubba would have been back there," I said. "A couple of people have said the leprechaun was lazy. So even if he didn't know the exact time he would be on a break, I have a hunch he was going back there to take a smoke break frequently, and Jake would have known that."

"You've got a point," Christy said. "I love when you notice things like that."

"I love when you both keep your noses out of my investigation," Ethan said with a sigh. "I'll talk with Jake and Sabrina again."

I nodded. "What else is going on, Ethan?" I asked and picked up my glass of tea. "Is there anyone else you've been talking to?"

"I wouldn't tell you if I had been talking to anybody else," he said and winked at me.

"What about security cameras?" I asked.

He shook his head. "Unfortunately, Jake never installed any security cameras in the alley. He said he intended to get some put up, but he never got around to it."

"I'm sure with all the work that they had to do to get the pub opened, that could have been overlooked," I said.

He nodded and took another sip of his iced tea. "I'm sure that's what happened."

The cameras may have been overlooked, but I was wondering if Sabrina lied about them being home the whole evening. Jake had admitted to Ethan that he was there at the pub. Why didn't she mention that? Of course, it's not like she had to mention it to us. We had just been having a casual conversation, and maybe she didn't even think about it. Maybe she meant that he had been at the pub earlier in the day, but they had taken the evening off.

"I'm starving," Christy said. "Please tell me we get to eat soon."

"If the potatoes don't take too long, I think we'll be in fried chicken heaven in about thirty minutes or so."

She groaned. "Thirty minutes is a long time to wait. I'm starving."

"Eat an Apple," I told her. I glanced at Ethan. He was deep in thought.

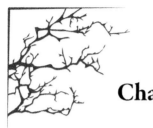

Chapter Seven

I PUSHED OPEN THE GIFT shop door and Christy and I stepped inside. Our friend Polly Givens owned the Pumpkin Hollow Gift Shop, and she had recently changed the décor to include plenty of shamrocks and leprechauns to celebrate the holiday. There were also a handful of jack-o'-lanterns and black cats hanging in the window. When you lived in a town that celebrates Halloween all year long, the Halloween décor never leaves the shops.

"Hello, Mia and Christy," Polly said as she headed over to us. "How are you two girls today?"

I smiled at her. "We're doing great, Polly. I ran out of candles, if you can believe it, and I thought I'd stop by and see what you had in stock."

She nodded. "Well, you came to the right place. I've already begun to get my Easter items in, and I've got lots of pretty pastel-colored candles. There's even a strawberry cheesecake scented one that I have fallen in love with."

"Strawberry cheesecake?" Christy asked with interest. "Oh my gosh, lead the way."

Polly chuckled, and we headed over to the display of candles. Polly always stocked the best-smelling candles in town, and I was addicted. I burned candles regardless of the season because I loved them so much, but my fall candles were all gone, and I had just finished the last Christmas cookie scented candle several days earlier. It was time to refresh my stock.

Polly picked up a pink candle and turned to us. "Take a smell of that and tell me what you think."

Christy took it from her and smelled it, inhaling deeply. She groaned. "Oh my gosh, this is the best candle ever."

She handed it to me, and I smelled it. Christy was right. It was more than just strawberry-scented; you could smell the undertones of cheesecake. "Yum. I've got to have one of these. What else have you got?"

Polly nodded and picked up a green candle and handed it to me. "That's mint chocolate chip."

I smelled it, and it was just as tasty smelling as the strawberry cheesecake. "Okay, I need this one, too."

Polly chuckled. "Well, I'm so glad you two stopped in. I'm going to sell a lot of candles this morning, aren't I?"

I nodded. "I'm afraid so."

She chuckled, then sobered. "I heard there was a murder at the new pub. What a shame."

I nodded. "Yes, we happened to be there when it happened that night."

"The leprechaun's luck ran out," Christy explained.

Polly shook her head. "You're awful, Christy."

"I am. I can't help it. It comes naturally to me."

We turned and looked as Sabrina Hall walked into the gift shop. She hesitated when she saw us, and then she smiled.

"Hello, ladies. How are you all doing today?"

"We're candle shopping, and we're delighted at what we have found," I told her.

"Candles? Oh, don't say that word. My husband will have a fit if I buy any more candles." She headed over to us and picked up a pale yellow candle, and smelled it. "Yum, lemon."

"Not just lemon," Polly pointed out. "Lemon meringue pie."

She smelled it again. "It smells so good. I've got to have this one. Like I said, don't tell my husband. He does not need to know about this."

"Your secret is safe with us," Polly told her. "I've got to unpack a box of picture frames over here, so if you ladies will excuse me, I'm going to get back to work."

"Thanks, Polly," I said. I turned to Sabrina. "You need to smell the strawberry cheesecake candle. It's wonderful."

Christy handed it to her, and she smelled it. "Gosh, this is good, too. Polly always has the best smelling candles in here. I'm supposed to be looking for a baby gift for my niece, but I can't pass the candles up."

"We could never pass them up, so we don't," I said.

She laughed. We looked over the candles, smelling each one, and Sabrina turned to us. "Mia, how is Ethan coming on the murder case?"

I glanced at her. "Oh, it's keeping him busy. He's always busy at the beginning of an investigation." I hoped she had something else to tell me. I wanted to know if they had really been home all evening like she had told us, but I couldn't bring it up without her wondering why I was asking.

She nodded. "I don't envy him his job, but I know he's good at it. You know, I was talking to Marissa Fields, and I have to wonder about her."

I picked up another candle and smelled it, and then looked at her. "Oh? What do you mean?"

She made a tsk-tsk sound and shook her head. "She's just so young. I told Jake when he hired her that she was too young for the job, but he insisted that she had waitressing experience and she would be fine. He wanted all of his employees to have some sort of food handling experience, so we hired her."

"I heard she was a waitress at a restaurant over in Truckee," Christy said. "She's not doing a good job for you?"

Sabrina hesitated and picked up another candle. "No, I guess she's doing a satisfactory job. But the more I think about things, the more I have to wonder about her. She seemed very friendly with Bubba."

"What do you mean, friendly?" I asked. I hadn't gotten a look at Bubba without his green makeup on, but I would've guessed he was in his forties, and Marissa was in her early twenties. Was she implying that there was some sort of relationship going on?

She nodded and set the candle down. "She's very flirtatious. I don't like flirtatious women. I think they cause issues with the rest of the staff, if you know what I mean. I saw her several times with Bubba sitting in a corner, giggling and whispering. It just makes me wonder."

"Did you ever ask either of them if anything was going on?" I asked. I wasn't sure I believed what she was telling me. Marissa was so much younger, and I was pretty sure she had a boyfriend. Why would she want to hang around with someone middle-aged?

She shook her head. "No. Maybe I'm jumping to conclusions, but it just seems so strange to me. A couple of the other waitresses pointed it out to me, too. But it's not like I could do anything about it, I'm not the boss there. And my husband, as I told you before, is kind of clueless about things. He was so busy trying to get the pub opened that he wouldn't notice something like that."

I nodded. "So you think they had a relationship?" I asked. "Do you think that she had something to do with Bubba's death?"

She eyed me. "I don't know. Like I said, maybe I'm jumping to conclusions. But why would she flirt with him the way she did? Maybe he did something that made her angry, and she killed him."

It did seem like she was jumping to conclusions, but I didn't say so. I wanted her to keep talking.

"She would've had to have gotten cleaned up pretty quickly," Christy pointed out. "I mean, the killer had to have gotten blood on their clothes when they slashed his throat. We saw her there that night, and she didn't have any blood on her."

Sabrina looked at her. "Yes, I suppose she would have. But what was to stop her from getting cleaned up? There's a hallway that runs from the backdoor to the staff restrooms. It wouldn't have been hard for her to do that. She could have been back at her post without anyone noticing anything."

She had a point. No one knew for sure how long Bubba had been laying back there. It probably hadn't been long, but even ten or fifteen minutes would have been plenty of time for the killer to have cleaned up in the bathroom as long as she hadn't gotten anything on her clothes. And then I wondered. Did she wear a black apron like some of the other staff wore?

"Do all the employees wear black aprons?" I asked her.

She turned to me and nodded, setting an orange candle back on the display. "Yes, all the staff wear a black apron. Jake decided that it was easier for everyone to keep clean that way." She sighed. "Now that you bring that up, I bet nobody stopped to check the garbage cans to see if there were any aprons that were thrown away. I bet that's what happened. I bet the killer took their black apron off and threw it away. Their clothes most likely would have been clean, and they could have grabbed a clean apron from the back."

"That's a possibility," I said thoughtfully. I hadn't thought about that. I needed to ask Ethan if all the garbage cans were checked before they were emptied.

She nodded. "Well, I guess I really don't know anything for certain, but these are the things that go through my mind late at night. I feel so terrible about Bubba losing his life. And Jake is just beside himself." She sighed. "Well, I had better get my candles paid for, and then I need to head to the grocery store. I might look for a baby gift online. It's good seeing you girls."

"It's good seeing you, too," I said as she headed up to the cash register to pay for her candles. I turned and looked at Christy, and she was watching Sabrina walk away. She looked at me, eyebrows raised.

I shrugged and picked up two candles. I could come back and get some more later. Christy picked up three, and we went to pay for them.

Chapter Eight

"I AM STARVING," CHRISTY said as I pulled into the parking lot at the pub.

"Me too. I'm glad the pub is open for lunch," I said. We parked and headed inside.

Jake and Sabrina didn't waste any time in reopening the pub after the murder. On the one hand, I could understand that because they had sunk so much money into getting it ready to open up, to begin with. But on the other hand, it was a family member that was killed here, and I would have thought they might have taken some more time off.

"They've got a good lunch crowd," Christy said, looking around. Most of the tables and booths were filled, and I wondered if it was because the food was so good, which it was, or if it was because people were interested that someone had been murdered here.

"They sure do," I agreed.

Marissa came up to us and smiled. "Hi Christy, hi Mia. Can I get you a table or booth?"

"A booth," I said.

She nodded and picked up two menus, and led us to a back corner booth. From where I sat, I had a view of the door that led to the kitchen. I glanced in that direction.

"So, how are things going?" I asked her as she laid the menus down in front of us.

She shrugged. "I guess it's been okay. Murder or not, it hasn't affected our business," she said, glancing around. "Can I get you something to drink?"

I nodded. "Iced tea, please."

Christy ordered the same, and she headed off to get our drinks while we looked over the menus.

"I think I'm going to go for a burger," Christy said, her eyes on the menu.

"Me too. I think I want a nice juicy cheeseburger." The pub had several cheeseburgers on the menu, and I was having a hard time deciding which one I wanted. The Ortega cheeseburger sounded good, and Ethan had really enjoyed it when we were here the other night. But they also had a western cheeseburger with a huge fried onion ring tucked between the bun and the beef patty.

I glanced up as a waitress headed back to the kitchen. The door swung open, and I could see the kitchen staff working. I wondered if one of them was the killer. But Bubba could have made enemies with someone in town, and they could have driven down the alley that night and killed him.

"Here we are," Marissa said. She set the glasses of iced tea in front of us. "Do you need a few more minutes?"

I shook my head. "No, I think I'm going to go with the western cheeseburger, and I'll take the wedge cut fries. I'm starving, and I'm pretty sure I can eat the whole thing." The western cheeseburger was huge, but I was pretty sure it was no match for my appetite.

Christy laid her menu on the corner of the table. "I think I'll have the same."

Marissa nodded and jotted down our orders. "I'll be right back with your food." She picked up the menus and headed back to the kitchen with our orders.

I looked at Christy. "I wonder how many people are here because there was a murder here, and they're curious."

She nodded. "I was thinking the same thing. People are so nosy around here. Not that I blame them," she said and chuckled. "I'm pretty nosy myself."

I nodded and looked up as Andy Hall headed toward us. He was Jake and Sabrina's son. When he saw us, he grinned. "Well, if it isn't the Jordan sisters. How are you two today?"

I nodded at him. "We're doing great. We're starving, and we knew that this was the place to come for the best food in town."

He chuckled. "Thank you for the compliment. We certainly have been working hard to earn that reputation. This place has been crazy busy since we opened."

"I bet," I said. "This is the second time I've been in here, and it's been packed both times."

"Devon and I have been here twice, too, and it was busy both times," Christy said. "I bet it keeps you guys running."

He nodded. "I tell you, when I get out of this place at night, I'm exhausted. But being busy also makes the time go quickly, so I guess I can't complain."

"Andy, we sure are sorry about what happened to your dad's cousin the other night," I said. "We were here for dinner. It's awful that he was murdered."

He sobered and nodded. "Yeah, it was a shock. I just can't believe it happened right here."

"Were you here that night? I can't remember seeing you." We had gone to school with Andy, and I was sure I would have noticed him had I seen him that night.

He shook his head. "No, I took the night off. It's been so busy here, and we've put in so many hours getting this place open that I needed a break."

"It must've been a shock when you heard about what happened." I took a sip of my iced tea.

His eyes widened. "I still can't believe it. My dad gave me a call late that night and told me what happened, and I made him repeat it three times because I just couldn't believe it."

I shook my head. "Do you have any idea who might have wanted to kill him?"

He hesitated. "I have no idea who might have killed him. Honestly, I had never met him before he came to work for us. My dad and he had been close when they were younger, so of course, when he found out that Bubba didn't have a job, he offered him one here. But I didn't like him. He was obnoxious and pushy."

"Really?" I asked. "You would think that since he was just starting a new job, he would have been easier to get along with."

"Exactly," Christy said. "Every time I start a new job, I'm always on my best behavior. I think most people are."

He snorted and shook his head. "Well, you would think so. But I guess because my dad owned the pub, he figured he could do as he pleased. It didn't make my dad happy, either."

"Oh?" I asked. "It bothered him?"

He nodded. "Yeah, it bothered him. Bubba was always ordering the rest of the staff around, and of course, that made them angry. My dad got a lot of complaints about him, and I know he and my mom were talking about letting him go."

This surprised me. Why didn't his mother tell me that? "It was that bad?"

He nodded. "Yeah, people got to where they just couldn't stand him anymore. I mean, if he would have asked people nicely and not been so bossy and pushy, people probably would have been fine with it. He wasn't the boss, but he behaved as if he was."

"That must have been hard for your father. To feel like he needed to fire him," Christy said and took a sip of her iced tea.

He glanced over his shoulder and then looked back at us. "Yeah, it was something he really didn't want to have to deal with. My mom told him that he needed to do it sooner rather than later just to get it over and done with. But my dad said he was going to have a talk with him first and see if he could get him to stop."

I sat back in my seat, thinking this over. "And did it? Did it help when he talked to him?"

He shrugged. "Honestly, I don't know if he ever got around talking to him. I meant to ask him, but then Bubba ended up dead, and I guess it just slipped my mind."

"Did his behavior change before he died?" Christy asked.

He shook his head. "No, I worked with him the night before he died, and he was ordering me around." He snorted again and shook his head. "Can you believe it? There's no way I was taking orders from him. My dad owns this place, and Bubba wasn't going to give me orders. So I'm assuming my dad never got a chance to talk to him, or if he did talk to him, it didn't make any difference."

"That's a shame," I said. "He sounded like a difficult person to work with, and since he was your dad's cousin, I'm sure it upset him that he was going to have to tell him to knock it off, or he was going to have to let him go."

"Yeah, my dad wasn't happy about it at all. The longer it went on, the angrier he got. Bubba was hired before we opened. He had actually been working here for about three months while we were getting the pub ready. He was ordering around the construction workers that were doing the remodel on the inside of the building."

"He was ordering them around, too?" Christy asked.

He nodded. "Yeah, I guess it was just his personality. He was a control freak."

I shook my head. "That's crazy that he would do that."

He grinned. "Right? Well, I better get going. I've got so much to do around here. It's good seeing you girls and catching up for a minute. I'll see you next time you're in."

"All right, Andy," I said. "It's good seeing you, and we will talk to you again soon."

We waited until he was out of earshot, and we looked at each other. "So Bubba was a control freak here at work," Christy said.

I nodded. "And nobody seemed to like him much. I wonder if he ordered somebody around one time too many, and they finally had enough and did away with him."

"I'm betting that's what happened," Christy agreed. "It also makes me wonder if maybe Jake did get a chance to talk to him, and they got into an argument when he tried to tell him that he couldn't order people around anymore."

She had a point. Bubba sounded like the sort of person that wasn't going to be told what to do, and if Jake had told him that he couldn't behave the way that he had been, then maybe they'd gotten into an argument over it, and Jake killed him. I could see Bubba becoming angry if his job was threatened, and the two of them arguing about it.

Chapter Nine

"I LOVE THE SMELL OF this place," Cindy Jennings said as she stood in the middle of the candy shop and inhaled. "I just can't get enough of this place."

"Cindy! How have you been?" I said coming out from behind the counter. "It's been forever since I've seen you." Cindy was a friend from high school, and I hadn't seen her in years.

She nodded and came over and hugged me. "I've missed you, Mia. I'm home visiting my parents for a couple of weeks, and I thought I'd stop in and buy far more candy than I need."

I chuckled. "A couple of weeks? You're taking your vacation in Pumpkin Hollow?"

She nodded and chuckled. "Sort of. My mom threw her back out, so I told my dad I would come and stay with them and help out around the house and help with my mom."

"Oh no," I said. "That sounds bad. I'm sorry."

She shrugged. "The doctor says she'll be good as new with some rest, but she will probably need surgery at some point. Her back has been bothering her for years, and now and then it goes out, and she can't get around very well. It gets better, and she won't have any issues for a few months or even a couple of years, but it always goes out again."

I shook my head and headed back to the front counter. "I hate to hear that. I bet it's miserable when it goes out, and she probably has no idea when it's going to happen."

She went to the display case and looked in at the fudge. "It is miserable for her, but I think it's not knowing when it's going to happen that bothers her the most. The doctor said she could have surgery, and she probably wouldn't have any more issues."

"When is she going to have the surgery?"

"Not for a couple more months. I suppose I'll be back in town then. That mint chocolate chip fudge looks good."

"It's really tasty. My mom made it in honor of St. Patrick's Day. Let me get you a sample."

I pulled the tray of fudge from the display case and cut her a small piece, handing it to her on a piece of waxed paper.

"Thank you so much," she said and popped it into her mouth. She smiled. "This is so good, Mia. I better get half a pound. My mother is just going to be lying around in bed so she may as well have some fudge to keep her happy."

"You can tell her it's a consolation prize for being in pain." I got to work cutting a half-pound piece of fudge for her mother and then wrapped it and put it into a bag. "How have you been?"

She shrugged. "I'm okay. I kind of miss Pumpkin Hollow. Every time I come home, I think, why don't I just move back? But of course, there's the problem of a job."

I nodded. "Exactly. If my mom didn't own the candy store, I don't know what I would do. Jobs around here are kind of in short supply."

"I know, it's like everybody who owns a business hires their relatives." She sighed. "Why couldn't my parents own some kind of Halloween-themed business?"

I chuckled. "Right? That has made life easier for Christy and me. Is there anything else you'd like?"

She took a look at the truffles in the display case. "What about those peppermint cream truffles? I love dark chocolate and peppermint. I think I'll take a half dozen of those. Your mom makes the best candy."

"Thanks," I said and went back to the display case and opened it up. "I have to agree with you. I don't know what we're going to do when she decides to retire."

"Do you and Christy make candy too?"

I nodded, pulling the tray out, and brought it over to the counter to put the truffles into another paper bag for her. "We both make candy, but I swear that my mother's candy is better. Either we had better improve our candy-making skills, or she is not allowed to retire."

She chuckled. "She may not like that idea."

"That's what I've been thinking." I placed six truffles into a smaller four-leaf clover printed paper bag and folded the top over.

"So, Mia, I heard there was a murder at that new pub. Isn't it crazy?"

I glanced at her. "Yeah, they killed the leprechaun. I still can't believe it."

She nodded. "That leprechaun was something else. I've been in the pub a couple of times since I got back, and he kept coming over to my table and flirting with me."

I stopped and looked at her. "Seriously? While he was on the job, he was coming to your table and flirting with you?"

She nodded, one eyebrow raised. "It was weird. I first I thought he was kind of cute with that Irish brogue, but he was way older than me, and honestly, I had no interest in him. But he kept coming to my table."

I shook my head. "That's kind of obnoxious. I mean, he's supposed to be working, and he's flirting with customers? So unprofessional."

She nodded. "He was just odd. He kept making these comments about me being pretty. It was just, I don't know, weird. It was over the top weird."

I hesitated. "Somebody might have taken offense to something like that." I leaned on the counter. "Maybe he flirted with the wrong person."

She nodded. "Wouldn't surprise me. As far as he was concerned, I was a stranger, and I was just going in there for lunch, and yet he was all over me. One of the barmaids came by, and she made a comment to him, telling him that he better get back to his post. He didn't like that at all."

I looked at her. "A barmaid? Do you remember which one it was?"

She shook her head. "No, I didn't know her. She was young and had blond hair." She shrugged. "I figured she'd seen enough of him acting that way with other customers, and she had just had enough of it."

Now that was odd. Sabrina had said that Marissa Fields and Bubba were giggling and flirting at a corner table. Was Marissa jealous when she saw him flirting with Cindy? None of it made sense because Marissa was so much younger than he was, and I couldn't imagine why she would have an interest in him. But stranger things have happened.

"Is there anything else you wanted? You had better get all the candy you want while you're here in town."

She glanced around the candy shop and shook her head. "No, I think that'll do it for now. But you can bet I'll be back in to get some more candy before I leave town. In fact, I might be in several more times." She chuckled.

I nodded. "It's been good seeing you, Cindy. Maybe we can get together and go to lunch before you leave?"

She nodded. "I would love that. We need to catch up."

She paid for her candy and left. Cindy and I had been close during high school, but we had drifted apart when we'd gone to different colleges. It would be fun to spend some time with her before she left.

I wiped down the glass countertop and took a look inside the display case. We needed more peanut butter fudge and peppermint patties.

The bell over the door jingled, and Ethan walked into the shop. He inhaled deeply. "This place smells so good."

"You have no idea how many times I hear that every day. And you just missed Cindy Jennings. Did you see her out front?"

He shook his head. "No, I haven't seen Cindy in ages."

"You must have just missed her. She's in town helping her mom. Her mom's back went out, and hopefully, I'm going to get to spend some time with her before she leaves."

He headed over to me and kissed me. "That sounds like fun. But I need some fudge."

"Why am I not surprised?" I said as he went to the display case and looked in.

"I'm going to have to have some of that mint chocolate chip fudge. I know your mom isn't going to be making it much longer, so I had better get my fill while I can."

"Yeah, you better," I advised and went to the display case and pulled the tray out again. "So what's going on? How is the investigation going?" Mom, Christy, and Linda Reid were in the kitchen making candy, and we were the only ones in the candy store.

He shrugged and leaned on the front counter. "I don't know, the more I hear about this leprechaun, the more I find that people really didn't like him. Aren't leprechauns supposed to be jolly souls? Aren't people supposed to like them?"

I shook my head and laughed. "Apparently not this one. Cindy said that she's been into the pub a couple of times, and he was all over her."

His eyebrows shot up. "All over her? At a place of business?"

I nodded. "That's what she said. He was flirtatious and obnoxious. She said the barmaid didn't like it one bit, and she told him to get back to work. Cindy doesn't know which barmaid it was, but she said she was young and blond, so I'm guessing it was Marissa."

He thought about this for a moment. "That's weird behavior. I mean, he's an employee, and he's flirting with the customers? I can see where that would make some people mad."

"Like Jake and Sabrina," I said. "Oh, and Andy." I filled him in on what Andy had told Christy and me the day before. I'd completely forgotten about it and hadn't told him what had happened.

He was quiet for a moment. "Well, there are several people who may have been annoyed enough with the leprechaun to have argued with him, but kill him? I don't know. I can't imagine getting so irritated with a coworker that they would do that."

"You've obviously never had really bad coworkers. There was a girl I worked with years ago while I was still in college, and I might have considered homicide a couple of times."

He narrowed his eyes at me. "I knew I needed to keep my eye on you."

I shrugged. "It's not like I have a bad temper or anything, but when you're picked on constantly, day after day, it gets to you. And since he'd been there for a couple of months working with everyone, I can see where someone might have been irritated with him enough to kill him."

I handed him the fudge, and he grinned. "My favorite. Thanks. And I guess I can see what you're saying. There's no telling who he might have made angry, and they just had enough of him."

"Ethan, were the garbage cans checked the night Bubba was killed? There's a hallway that leads to the employee restrooms, and Sabrina said the killer could have gone back there to clean up. She wondered if Marissa killed Bubba. She said she might have ditched her black apron in the garbage if it had blood on it."

He nodded. "Garbage cans were checked, and no evidence was found."

I sighed. "It was a thought."

He kissed me. "It was a very good thought, too. I've got to go."

"I'll see you later."

An angry co-worker was probably our best bet as the killer, but if Bubba was as flirtatious as Cindy had said he was, then maybe he had pushed someone else in Pumpkin Hollow too far.

Chapter Ten

"THE NEXT MORNING, CHRISTY and I stopped off at the bakery to pick up some donuts for everyone at the candy store. We had plenty of sugar at the candy store, but we couldn't resist the donuts. Plus, we were going to buy some coffee, and who doesn't love coffee?

We got in line behind a woman who was buying four dozen donuts, and we waited. Angela Karis was behind the front counter, and she leaned past the customer to greet us. "Good morning, Christy. Good morning, Mia. How are you girls today?"

"We're doing well," I said. "We're in the mood for donuts, so we had to make a stop."

She nodded. "There's nothing like a fresh donut in the morning."

"That's right, and that's why I needed four dozen," the woman at the counter said and laughed. "Honestly, they're not all for me. I'm bringing them to work."

"Oh, we believe you," Angela said with a wink. "But we wouldn't judge, even if you were taking them all home. We love our donuts."

"You can say that again," Christy agreed.

The woman paid for her donuts and then picked up the stack of four boxes and peered over them to make her way to the front door. "I hope I don't drop these."

"Let me help you," Christy said and hurried to the front door and opened it for her.

"That's so sweet of you," the customer said as she turned sideways to get the boxes through the door.

I headed up to the front counter and looked into the display case. "Everything looks so good. Why don't you just give me a dozen of assorted donuts? Oh, but make sure there's at least one lemon-filled donut. I love those."

Angela nodded and picked up a bakery box and unfolded it. "The lemon-filled donut is one of my favorites, too. So how are you doing, Mia? How's married life treating you?"

I grinned. "I think I'm going to enjoy married life. I like having Ethan around all the time. Well, when he's not at work, that is."

She nodded. "Yeah, I was married once, and I enjoyed it too. Until I didn't. That was right about the time that I found out my husband was cheating on me." She shrugged. "But that doesn't mean I wouldn't try it again. Married life, I mean."

I nodded. "You may as well give it another try. Practice makes perfect."

She chuckled and opened up the display case door. "That's something to keep in mind. Say, Mia, I heard there was a murder at the new pub. Is that right?"

I nodded as Christy came to stand beside me. "Yes, the leprechaun was murdered."

She chuckled. "You're not serious, are you?"

I nodded. "His luck ran out. And I've got to stop making stupid bad luck jokes."

She nodded. "It's a pure shame is what it is. A leprechaun isn't even safe in his own pub."

"That leprechaun died with his little curly-toed boots on," Christy said.

She shook her head. "Well I heard a rumor," she said, looking at me, one eyebrow raised. She didn't continue, and I knew that she wanted me to ask. I hated to ask because Angela thrived on gossip. But if she knew something, then I needed to know what that something was.

"What did you hear?" I asked reluctantly.

"I heard he and that cute blond barmaid were an item."

This wasn't the first time I had heard that, but I didn't believe it. I just couldn't see Marissa with Bubba. "Who told you that?"

She shrugged and put two lemon-filled donuts into the box. "It gets around. You know how this town is. Apparently, the minute that leprechaun came to town, the two of them were an item."

"But there was at least a twenty-year age difference between them. Maybe twenty-five years," Christy pointed out. "I just can't see it."

She shrugged and picked up two sprinkle donuts and put them into the box. "They were an unlikely couple, but from what I hear, Marissa wanted to get married."

"And?" I said when she didn't continue.

She closed the display case door and opened up the one next to it. "So I heard she wanted the leprechaun to marry her. Like, desperately."

"Why would she want that?" Christy asked, leaning on the front counter. "Marissa is a cute girl. I thought she had a boyfriend. One closer to her age."

Angela shrugged. "The last person I heard she was going out with was Dave Cauffman. They got into an argument because he wanted her to move in with him, but she wanted him to marry her. And because he refused to marry her, she broke it off and went looking for someone else."

"Why would she want to be married that desperately?" I asked. "I mean, it seems like she would be a little choosy about who it was that she was trying to marry."

"Yeah, you would think so, wouldn't you? But I tell you, the rumors are flying. They said that she was so desperate to marry that as soon as she laid eyes on that leprechaun, she tried to get him to ask her out, and she was determined to get him to marry her. He was the pub owner's cousin, after all, and if she was with him, she might get preferential treatment. Maybe she'd make more money than the other barmaids."

I wasn't sure I believed it. But then I remembered what Cindy said about Bubba making passes at her. If what Angela was saying was true, then maybe Marissa got jealous and killed Bubba. But I still didn't think it could be true.

"There are plenty of single guys that are closer to her age in this town," Christy pointed out. "Why wouldn't she want to be with one of them? Shoot, it would've made more sense if she would have made a pass at Andy Hall. He's the pub owner's son, and he has a bigger stake in the pub than the owner's cousin would have. Plus, he's good-looking. Why wouldn't she make eyes at him?"

Angela looked over the top of her glasses at Christy. "Andy Hall? He's engaged to Kimberly Adams. He's a good guy from what I hear, and the two of them are supposed to get married this summer. It wouldn't surprise me if Marissa threw herself at him, and when she realized she wasn't going to get anywhere with him, she went after the leprechaun."

"Rumors in this town are a dime a dozen," I said. "And I do not see Marissa and Bubba being a couple. I just can't see it."

She stopped a moment, a chocolate bar in one hand.

"It's hard for me to believe it too, but I saw the two of them together at a restaurant. They were back in a corner, and they seemed very chummy. Like, chummier than a working relationship."

I glanced at Christy. Her brow was furrowed. "You saw them? With your own eyes?"

She put the chocolate bar into the box and nodded. "Yes, with my own eyes. I'm telling you, she was giggling and laughing and really enjoying herself. Look, someone was paying attention to her. What's wrong with that? Lots of women date older men. Lots of older women date younger men. There's no rule against any of that."

She was right, as much as I hated to admit it. There was no rule against it. I just couldn't see the two of them together. "Okay. So maybe they were seeing one another. But what does that mean? Just because they were seeing each other doesn't mean she would kill him." Was she holding out on me? Did she know more?

She shrugged and put two maple bars into the donut box. "It doesn't prove anything. But it's something for Ethan to look into. Bubba didn't know many people in this town since he hadn't lived here long, right? So it makes sense that it would be somebody that knew him. Somebody that was around him quite a bit."

I crossed my arms in front of me. I hated when Angela had a point. "All right, I'll certainly mention all of this to Ethan. It won't hurt to let him know about it."

She nodded and finished filling the box with donuts. "He just needs to keep an open mind while he's looking into this investigation. Just because it doesn't seem likely doesn't mean that it isn't likely. I've got a hunch about this one."

I nodded and paid for the donuts. "Thanks for the donuts, Angela. We'll see you later."

She nodded as we headed to the front door. "And don't be a stranger. Let me know what Ethan thinks about my theory. I'm telling you, she's guilty."

"Goodbye, Angela!" I called over my shoulder as we headed out to my car.

"What do you think?" Christy asked me when the door closed behind us.

"I think that Angela listens to too much gossip. Like I said, I'll mention it to Ethan, but as far as I'm concerned, it's all gossip."

Angela was the queen of Pumpkin Hollow gossip. But that didn't mean that at least part of it wasn't right. It was just figuring out which part was right.

Chapter Eleven

LATER THAT DAY I WAS refilling the bulk candy bins. I looked up when the candy store door opened, and Jake Hall walked in and smiled at me.

"Hello, Mia," he said with a nod. "How are you this afternoon?"

I closed the lid to the jellybean bin and sighed. "Busy. You would think St. Patrick's Day isn't a big candy buying holiday, but we sure have been busy. How are you doing?"

He hesitated, looking around the store for a moment, and then turned back to me. "I guess I'm all right. As all right as I can be, anyway. I suppose you heard about my cousin?"

I nodded. "Yes, Ethan and I were there at the pub the night he died. I'm so sorry for your loss."

He shoved his hands into his jeans pockets and nodded. "That's right. Ethan told me you were having dinner there, and you dropped by with some candy the other day. Sorry, it's still such a shock, and I'm not thinking straight. I mean, he's gone. I guess it sounds crazy since it's been over a week now, but I just can't believe it. I called his mom the other night, and she cried the entire time I was on the phone. I felt so bad for her."

"Oh, that's so sad. I'm sorry. I can't imagine what it must be like to have a child die. It has to be devastating." I headed over to the front counter and went behind it. "You tell her that we sure are sorry about what happened to him."

He nodded and followed me to the front counter and stopped in front of the display case, glancing in. "Yeah, it's awful. His body was shipped back to Ohio for the funeral, you know. I'm going to fly out next week to attend."

I nodded. "I guess all of his immediate family is in Ohio?"

He nodded. "Yeah, after he moved there, his parents moved there, too."

"Did he have any kids?" I asked, leaning on the counter.

He shook his head. "No, he never had any kids. He was married once when he was in his twenties, but the marriage only lasted three years, and they never had any kids."

"I feel bad for you and the entire family." I wondered if he would bring up what his son had said about him wanting to fire Bubba. I'm sure that it had to have been a difficult situation for him, and even if he did feel he needed to let him go, that didn't mean that he didn't care about his cousin. Working with family could be tricky sometimes.

He glanced in at the display case again. "I think I want to pick up half a pound of the mint chocolate chip fudge. I've been thinking about your mother's fudge for a few days now. We sure appreciated what you brought by the other day."

I nodded and went to the back of the display case and opened it up. "You're certainly welcome. It always feels inadequate to bring somebody candy after somebody's death, but it feels like we should do something for them, you know?"

He nodded. "Sure, I can understand that. And it's appreciated that you thought about us."

I weighed out the fudge and wrapped it for him. "Is there anything else I can get you?"

He glanced around the shop and then shook his head. "No, I think I'll be back in and pick up some candy for Bubba's mom and dad when I get ready to go to the funeral. But I'll wait and do that the day before I go."

I nodded. "It'll be fresher that way." I slipped the fudge into a paper bag and then glanced at him again. "Jake, do you have any idea who might have killed your cousin?"

He looked at me intently, jingling the change in his pockets. "To be honest? I have to wonder about Marissa. The two of them were awfully chummy."

I rang up his order. "So you think Marissa might have done it? Why do you think that?"

He shrugged and pulled some money out of his pocket and laid it on the counter. "I don't know. There's just something about her that bothers me. Look at the age difference between the two of them. It's not like Bubba had money or anything at all besides the job that I gave him. I never understood why she had such an interest in him."

I took the money and put it into the cash register. "It's hard to say why somebody might be attracted to someone else. There's no telling, I guess."

He nodded. "Yeah, I guess that's true. You never know who someone might be attracted to. And sometimes it's not like you get much of a choice." He chuckled. "I took one look at my wife thirty years ago, and I fell in love instantly. I'm pretty sure that people thought she was too good for me, but she decided that she loved me right back."

I smiled. "That's sweet. I mean the part about just falling in love with her, and she fell in love with you back. I bet nobody thought she was better than you, though. I'm sure they were happy for you."

He shrugged. "Maybe so. Maybe so." He got quiet and looked away.

"Were you and Bubba close?"

He turned and looked at me again and smiled sadly, then nodded. "Yeah, when we were kids, we were inseparable. We did everything together, and I thought we would always be the best of friends. But then we went our separate ways after we got out of high school, and you know how life is. It takes you to different places. When I heard he was out of a job, the first thing I thought was that I could offer him one here at the pub that I was opening, and then we could hang out together again. I was really looking forward to that."

"I'm sorry that was cut short," I said. "That must be very difficult." My heart went out to Jake. He seemed genuinely sad about bubba's death.

"It is. I honestly didn't think something like this would happen. And I guess maybe I shouldn't say that about Marissa, but there's just something about her. She was always hanging all over him, and she was also very pushy. Always telling him what to do."

"She was?"

He nodded. "Yeah, it was weird. It was like she couldn't stand it unless she was telling him what to do."

"I guess some people are like that. She probably didn't mean anything by it," I said, straightening up a display of lollipops on the counter.

"Yeah, maybe she didn't mean anything by it. Maybe she didn't realize what she was doing, but it bothered me that she was so controlling."

"Really? Why do you think he put up with it? Did you ever mention it to him?"

He nodded. "Yeah, I asked him one day why he didn't just tell her to mind her own business, but he laughed and said that was just Marissa. It was just the way she was."

"So they were actually dating?"

He shrugged. "I honestly don't know. I don't think they were actually dating, but she sure wanted to."

"But Bubba didn't?"

He hesitated again. "I don't know if I could say that Bubba didn't want to. I think maybe it was just a case of we had so much work to do to get the pub opened that he didn't have the time. I'm sure once things had settled down, if he was really interested in her, he would have asked her out."

"I'm sure it was very hard putting in all those hours to get the pub opened up."

"Oh yeah, you have no idea. I was worried we wouldn't get it opened before St. Patrick's Day, but everything came together, and we got it opened in time."

"I think having him dress as a leprechaun there at the pub was clever."

He laughed. "That was his idea. He did a great Irish brogue imitation, and so he thought it would be fun if he dressed as a leprechaun and painted his face green. I thought it was a great idea to draw customers into the pub, and it worked like a charm."

I nodded. "It was a lot of fun. You couldn't have convinced me that he wasn't actually Irish. But then when I found out that his name was Bubba, that kind of gave me a hint that he wasn't from Ireland."

He laughed again. "Yeah, an Irish leprechaun named Bubba? I guess that doesn't happen often."

I grinned. "It would have been a lot of fun having him hang around, I'm sure."

"Yeah, he had the gift of gab. He could keep people entertained with that accent of his." He picked up the bag of fudge on the counter. "Well, Mia, it's been nice talking to you. I'll see you later."

I nodded. "See you later, Jake."

I watched as he headed out of the candy store. He hadn't mentioned the fact that he was going to fire him. But maybe he never got around to telling Bubba, or maybe he had changed his mind. And maybe it was something that he didn't want to think about now that Bubba had died.

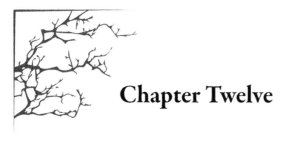

Chapter Twelve

"LOOK AT YOU," I SAID to Ethan as he walked into the candy store. "Two days in a row. I am the luckiest woman in the entire world."

He snorted and shook his head. "Well, you just may be the luckiest woman in the world, but I'm an even luckier man." He leaned over and kissed me and then pulled me to him. "Just don't tell anybody I'm here at the candy store this often. No one needs to know how much candy I actually eat every week."

I chuckled and went behind the front counter. "Your secret is safe with me. What can I get for you?"

He looked into the display case. "You know me so well. What about the crème de menthe fudge? Why don't I try some of that?"

I nodded. "Mom's been experimenting with the recipe. She's not happy with it, so we didn't put it online to sell, but I think she's just being a perfectionist. It's pretty tasty." I reached into the display case and pulled out the tray of fudge and cut a big piece for him, and slid it across the counter on a piece of waxed paper. "Tell me what you think about it."

He took a bite of it and nodded. "Excellent. Your mother has nothing to worry about."

I chuckled. "Maybe she'll believe it when it comes from you, but not from me."

"I'll tell her myself," he said, turning to the kitchen as my mother walked out with a tray of green four-leaf clovers made from tinted white chocolate.

"Ethan," she said, smiling. "It's so good to see you today."

He nodded and held up the piece of fudge. "This is excellent fudge. You don't need to do a thing to the recipe. Honestly, this may become my new favorite."

"Ethan, you're just saying that." She came around behind the front counter, and I stepped aside so she could put the four-leaf clovers into the display case.

"I told you so," I said to Ethan. "She's a perfectionist."

She chuckled. "Maybe I am. But I just feel like that recipe needs a little more tweaking before I'm satisfied with it."

"You can tweak it all you want, but it's pretty darn good," Ethan told her. He looked at the tray she held. "What are those you have there?"

"These are white chocolate four-leaf clovers. I put a creamy vanilla center in them. Of course, it's white chocolate dyed green."

"They sound tasty," he said.

She picked up a piece of waxed paper and slid two of them across the counter to him. "You had better try them out to make sure they're tasty."

He grinned. "I'll be your candy tester any day."

She chuckled and closed the display case door. "I'll take you up on that. I've got some peanut butter fudge that I'm in the middle of making right now, so I had better get back to the kitchen before it sets up on me."

"It was good seeing you again, Ann," Ethan said.

"You too, Ethan. You need to come over for dinner sometime soon." She headed back to the kitchen with the empty tray.

"I'll take you up on that offer," he called after her and turned back to me. "I love your mom."

I chuckled. "Me too." We both turned toward the door when it opened, and Doug Fazio from the pub walked in.

He grinned. "Well, if it isn't Ethan and Mia Banks. Imagine running into you two here."

"I'm sure you've got to be in shock," I said sarcastically. We'd gone to school with Doug, and we knew him fairly well. Now he had a job as one of the dishwashers at the pub. "What's going on, Doug?"

He shrugged and sauntered up to the front counter and leaned on it next to Ethan. "Not a lot. I've got the day off, and I decided to make the rounds of Pumpkin Hollow. I paid a couple of bills, bought some groceries, and now I thought I'd stop in and get some candy."

I nodded. "It's a good thing you did. Ethan here was going to eat all we had. I'm glad you're here to stop him."

Ethan groaned. "I don't eat that much candy, Mia." He looked at me, one eyebrow raised.

I looked at Doug and shrugged. "So he says. What can I get you, Doug?"

He glanced at the display case. "How about some regular fudge with walnuts?"

"You got it," I said. "You're sure you don't want to try any of the St. Patrick's Day flavors?"

He shook his head. "No, I think I just want some good old-fashioned chocolate fudge with walnuts."

"You got it," I said and took out the tray. "How much?"

"Half a pound. I'm celebrating my day off."

I nodded and chuckled. "Coming right up."

He turned and looked at Ethan. "So Ethan, how is the investigation going? Have you found the leprechaun killer yet?"

Ethan shook his head. "Not yet, but I'm sure it won't be long. I bet everybody's shaken up there at the pub, aren't they?"

He nodded. "Yeah, everybody's pretty shaken up. It was kind of surreal finding a dead leprechaun on your back step."

Ethan nodded. "I'm sure it was."

He frowned. "You know, that Bubba, he was a real jerk. Not that I would wish death on him, of course, but I'm not sorry that I don't have to work with him anymore."

"What do you mean?" Ethan asked him.

He shrugged. "He thought because his cousin owned the pub that he could order people around. And he wasted no time in doing that. And honestly, he was just miserable to have to work with. Have you ever worked with somebody that thinks they're the boss when they're anything but?"

Ethan shook his head. "No, I don't think so."

"Ethan has only had positive work experiences," I informed Doug. "But believe me, I have had some very unpleasant work experiences. That, of course, was in my past while I was still in college, so I understand what you're saying."

He nodded and chuckled. "I'm glad somebody understands me."

"Maybe I just know how to get along with people," Ethan suggested, giving me a look.

I shook my head and turned to Doug. "So, it was miserable working with Bubba the leprechaun?"

He nodded. "I don't know, maybe he would have settled down at some point, but it was rough, let me tell you. He and Andy Hall couldn't get along. The two of them argued a lot."

"Oh?" Ethan asked, turning to him. "What did they argue about?"

Doug shrugged. "I guess the usual stuff. He tried to order Andy around, and Andy wasn't having it. Not that I blame him. One day they were out back, and we heard them yelling at each other. Honestly, I thought it was going to come to blows. We all hurried to the back door, and we watched them for a few minutes. They didn't know we were watching at first, but then they turned and looked at us. That kind of broke it up. But I tell you, they were mad."

"Because Bubba was ordering Andy around? Or was it something else?" Ethan asked.

"I only heard a little of the argument, but Bubba said he was going to make sure that his dad fired him."

This surprised me. "That takes a lot of nerve," I said. "I mean, he's the boss's son. Why on earth would he think he could get Jake to fire Andy?"

He chuckled and nodded. "Right? That's what I was thinking. But it almost seemed like Bubba had something on him. I don't know if he did or not, but it kind of felt that way to me."

"I wonder what he might have had on him," I said, glancing at Ethan. I wrapped up Doug's fudge and put it into a bag.

Doug shrugged. "Honestly, maybe I'm reading more into it than there was because I didn't hear a lot. There was a lot of shouting going on, and the two did not get along. Ever."

I rang up his fudge. "That sounds odd if it's true that he thought he had something on Andy and could get his dad to fire him."

"Maybe I should have another talk with Andy," Ethan said carefully. "Is there anything else you can think of that might be of interest?"

Doug hesitated, then he shook his head and paid for his fudge. "No, not really. I'm just glad I don't have to deal with him anymore. Now that doesn't mean that I am glad he's dead, like I said earlier, but things are a lot quieter at the pub now."

"I bet," Ethan said.

He picked up his bag of fudge. "Well, it's been good seeing you two. Now I've got to go home and eat this entire slab of fudge."

I eyed him. "All of it? At once? You'll get sick."

He shrugged. "It's worth the risk." He chuckled and headed to the door.

"See you later, Doug," Ethan said.

"See you," he said and headed out the door.

I turned to Ethan. "What do you think about that?"

He shrugged. "He isn't certain about what was being said."

I nodded. "Jake was in here earlier, and he said he was really sad about his cousin getting killed. But his son had told us that he was supposed to fire Bubba. Jake never brought that up."

"Could be he's embarrassed about it now," Ethan said. "Maybe he feels bad for considering firing him."

I nodded. "It's a possibility. But it does make me wonder. Maybe he's hoping that no one knew about it."

Ethan turned to me. "Maybe. It's hard to tell at this point." He leaned over and kissed me. "Thanks for the candy. I'll see you later tonight."

"I'll see you later."

I hoped Ethan found the leprechaun killer soon. Knowing a killer was on the loose made me nervous.

Chapter thirteen

"THERE'S MY SWEET GIRL," Christy said, holding her arms out to Isabella. We'd stopped by the coffee shop on our break for a little caffeine boost.

"I'm next," I told Christy as Amanda handed the baby across the counter to her.

Amanda chuckled. "You two are going to spoil that girl."

"That's our job," Christy said with a nod and kissed the baby on top of her head. "That's what babies are for, anyway. So you can't blame us."

"She's got a point," I said to Amanda. "Babies are meant to be spoiled."

She shook her head and chuckled. "All right, you can spoil her for now. But when she gets older, and she understands what being spoiled is all about, you two are going to have to take it easy. I don't want her to be a spoiled child."

I shrugged. "We will discuss that when the time comes." I looked up at the menu board. "I think I want a peppermint patty monster mocha."

Amanda nodded. "One peppermint patty monster mocha coming up. What about you, Christy?"

Christy eyed the chalkboard above Amanda. "I think I'm going to go with a vampire's kiss."

"One vampire's kiss coming up. Large?"

Christy nodded. "Oh yes. I need a large."

She got to work on our drinks and glanced at us. "So? It's St. Patrick's Day. What are you two going to do to celebrate?"

"Devon and I are going to have dinner at the pub. There's a darts tournament that he wants to enter," Christy said.

"That sounds like fun. What about you, Mia?"

"I'm going to make dinner and hope that Ethan can get off early enough to enjoy it with me."

"Aw, boo. Let's hope he does," Amanda said. "Brian and I are going to go to my mom's. She wants to see the baby."

"At least you won't have to cook," I said.

She nodded. "So, anything new? How is Ethan doing on the leprechaun murder case?"

I shrugged and leaned on the front counter, looking into the display case that held all the tasty baked goods Amanda sold. "He's still working on it. I'm sure he'll have a break in the case any time now." I hoped that was true. Killing a leprechaun seemed more cruel than just killing your average joe for some reason. The crime needed to be solved.

"I sure hope so," she said.

There were four-leaf clover sugar cookies in the display case, along with some cupcakes with green frosting. "What kind of cupcakes are those?"

She glanced at the display case. "Chocolate with green peppermint frosting. Want one?"

I shook my head. "No, but I think I'll take one of the four-leaf clover sugar cookies."

"I want one of those, too," Christy said.

Amanda nodded and kept working on our coffees. "I sure hope Ethan finds the leprechaun killer soon. I think that's what we should refer to them as. The leprechaun killer. Can you see the headlines in the newspaper? Leprechaun killer still at large."

I shook my head and smiled. "I'm sure Ethan would be thrilled with that headline."

"Well, he had better get on the ball and get that killer found if he doesn't want to see a headline like that," Christy said, bouncing the baby lightly in her arms.

I shrugged. "You know how it is. Killers never want to volunteer their names to the police."

Christy snorted. "That does make it a little harder."

When Amanda finished our coffees, Brian came out of the backroom.

He smiled at us. "Well, look who's here. I see you're spoiling my daughter again."

Christy nodded. "Of course I am. It's my job. Don't act so surprised."

"Yeah, yeah."

When we paid for our coffee and cookies, we headed to a corner table, and Amanda followed us over. She sat down in the chair across from us. "It's time for me to take a break, anyway. Brian can handle the front counter."

I nodded. "So what's new with you, Amanda? Anything going on?"

"Isabella has been cutting teeth. And she's not letting us get much sleep."

I looked over at Isabella. "Oh, poor, Isabella. I'm sure that's miserable for her."

She nodded. "She's drooling all over the place, too. I'll be glad when those teeth come in."

We looked up as the front door opened and Marissa Fields walked in. She looked over at us and smiled and then headed to the front counter to place an order with Brian.

Christy looked at me, one eyebrow raised, and I shrugged.

I took a sip of my coffee and turned back to Amanda. "So she's cutting teeth? She'll look so cute when she has teeth."

She nodded. "It's kind of funny to see her with that one front tooth now, but you can't see it unless she smiles really big."

Christy started bouncing her, and sure enough, Isabella smiled so she could see the tooth. She started laughing. "That is adorable. It's not all the way in yet." She turned the baby toward me, and I smiled at her.

"She's so sweet."

Marissa came over to our table when she had paid for her coffee. "Hi, everyone." She turned and looked at me before anyone could answer. "Mia, can I talk to you about something?"

I nodded, glancing at Amanda and Christy. "Sure. What is it?"

She hesitated. "Can I talk to you in private? There's something that I need to talk to Ethan about. About the case." She glanced at Christy and Amanda.

I got to my feet and picked up my coffee. "Let's go over here." We headed to a table at the other end of the room and sat down.

She took a sip of her coffee. "I found some letters."

I looked at her, one eyebrow raised. "Letters? What kind of letters?"

"Letters that Sabrina Hall had sent to Bubba when he was in Ohio."

This was interesting. I took a sip of my coffee. "How did you find them?"

She shrugged. "Before the pub opened, I needed some work, so I offered to do anything the Halls needed. I offered to come into the pub to clean it, and they said that they didn't need any help with that. But Sabrina said they could use some help with cleaning their house. They weren't home very much with all the work they were doing to open the pub, and she wanted me to come in and do some light dusting, vacuuming, and washing the dishes. Stuff like that. So I said yes because I couldn't stand sitting around my house anymore, and I needed the money."

I nodded. "So you saw some letters?" I wondered exactly where those letters were when she saw them. It sounded to me like she was snooping.

"Yes, I saw some letters. They were sitting right on the dresser. I wasn't snooping." Her eyes went wide as if she could read my mind.

I wasn't sure I believed her, but I had no reason not to believe her at this point. "So, the letters?"

She nodded. "I know I shouldn't have done it. So I guess at this point, I actually was snooping, but I read one of the letters.

It was a love letter. To Bubba, from Sabrina. She said it was nice talking to him the previous week and that she couldn't wait for him to come to California so they could be together."

This surprised me. "But I thought this was during the time when the pub was being built? I thought Bubba was already here at that time."

She nodded. "He was. Not for all of it though, just for a couple of months before the pub opened. They worked on the pub for about five months before it opened, and he got here right after Christmas."

I thought this over. "So where did you find the letters? In Sabrina's bedroom?"

She shook her head. "No, it was in Bubba's room. They were sitting right there on the dresser. If they had been in her room, her husband might have seen the letters and probably would have read them. He probably never went into Bubba's room."

"Why didn't you tell Ethan about this earlier?"

She hesitated. "I forgot about them, I guess. It didn't occur to me that they might be important, but I've been thinking it over, and maybe it is important."

"That's something that Ethan probably should know about," I said. I didn't believe her when she said she forgot about the letters or didn't think they were important. I wasn't sure if the letters themselves meant anything, but her not mentioning them before now might.

And when we had spoken to Sabrina, it seemed like she was anxious about getting rid of Bubba. Maybe they'd had a falling out. Or maybe Jake had caught on to the fact that they had eyes for one another. It made me wonder what kind of relationship they had.

She nodded. "I'm going to tell Ethan. As a matter of fact, I was on my way over to the police station now, and I just stopped in for a coffee. When I saw you, I thought I'd tell you. You won't talk to anybody else about it, will you?"

I shook my head. "No, I won't say a word to anyone. But definitely talk to Ethan. You didn't happen to keep any of the letters, did you?"

She shook her head. "No, I should have. There were five or six of them sitting there. I read two of them, and they both pretty much said the same thing. That she couldn't wait for him to move here."

I nodded. "Definitely talk to Ethan about them then. It's something that he needs to know."

She smiled and almost seemed relieved. "That's where I'm headed now. I'm going to go to the station and talk to him about it." She got to her feet. "Thanks, Mia. I'll see you later."

I nodded. "See you later, Marissa." I watched as she headed out the door. She said she didn't keep a copy of the letters, and since Bubba was dead, it wouldn't surprise me if Sabrina had gone into his bedroom to clear out his things. I had a hunch that the letters were no longer around.

Chapter fourteen

IT WAS LATER IN THE afternoon when I saw Ethan pull up to the curb in front of the candy store. I glanced over at Christy. "Christy, I'm going to step outside and say hello to Ethan."

She looked at me suspiciously. "Why do you need to go outside to talk to him?"

I hadn't told her about what Marissa had said to me earlier, and for the time being, I wasn't going to. She was suspicious, of course. I smiled. "I just want to say hello to my husband. I'll be right back."

She snorted. "Sure, that's all you're going to say to him."

"I promise," I said over my shoulder. She couldn't see that my fingers were crossed in front of me. I headed out the door before she had a chance to say anything else.

Ethan got out of his police-issue unmarked car and looked at me, surprised to see me coming to meet him outside. "Well, curbside service."

I grinned and went to him and kissed him. "Anything for the best husband in the whole world."

One eyebrow arched upward. "The best husband in the whole world? All right, I'm not going to argue with you about that. You've never been married before, so you have no idea whether I'm truly the best husband or not. We'll just let you believe it."

I chuckled and kissed him again. "How are things going?"

He shrugged. "What's going on with you? Why did you run out here to meet me? Looks suspicious to me."

"Looks suspicious?" I asked and lightly slapped him on the arm. "You're changing the subject without answering my question. You're more suspicious than I am."

He chuckled. "Well, if there's nothing suspicious going on and I'm going to get curbside service, where's the candy? You would have brought me candy."

I shook my head and snorted. "I was at the coffee shop earlier, and Marissa Fields came in. She said that the Halls had hired her to clean their house before the pub opened, and she just happened to run across some letters in Bubba's room. Letters from Sabrina."

His eyebrows shot up. "What do you mean? What kind of letters?"

I sighed. "She said she read two of them, and they were love letters from Sabrina and to Bubba. She sent them to him when he was in Ohio."

He stared at me. "Wait a minute, Sabrina was sending love letters to Bubba while he was in Ohio? But I thought the idea for him to come to work at the pub was Jake's idea?"

I nodded. "That's what I thought, too. Marissa said the letters said Sabrina could hardly wait for him to move to

California. She also said she was going right over to the station to talk to you about them. She never showed up?"

He shook his head. "I wasn't at the station this morning. I had some errands to run, and when I got back, I was in a meeting for a while."

I nodded. "Okay then, she might have tried to come to talk to you, and she probably didn't let anybody at the station know what she wanted. I'm suspicious about why she didn't say anything about the letters earlier. She said she didn't think it was important, but now she's decided that they might be."

"It would have been nice if she had mentioned them the first time I talked to her."

I nodded. "She said she left the letters in Bubba's room. And since he's been dead for over a week, I'm assuming that those letters aren't there anymore."

He sighed. "Because someone would have gathered up all of his things and sent them back to his parents."

"And if Sabrina was worried that the letters might still be around, she probably cleaned that room herself right after he died."

He took a step back and leaned against his car. "So maybe Jake found out about the relationship, and he killed him."

I nodded. "Or maybe Marissa got jealous of him flirting with other women, and she killed him. And now maybe she'd like to pin it on Sabrina."

"Maybe. But it would have been tough for Sabrina to watch Marissa throwing herself at Bubba and him reciprocating right there in front of her after she had written him love letters."

I leaned against the car next to him. "Or maybe Marissa's lying. Maybe there weren't any love letters, and she's making it up. Setting Sabrina up."

He crossed his arms in front of himself and was quiet for a moment. Then he nodded. "That's a possibility, too. Because if no one else knew about the letters, then it would be easy enough for her to make that up. Sabrina isn't going to volunteer that she wrote him love letters."

"Sabrina has said that Bubba was lazy. She's said that several times and she really hasn't been very positive about him. I have a feeling that the letters do exist, and she was jealous. She killed him because he was flirting with not only Marissa, but any female that walked into the pub. Remember what Cindy said? She didn't even know him, and he was flirting with her."

He nodded. "Sounds like Bubba really got himself into trouble with the women."

"And let's not forget that Marissa said Jake and Bubba argued about money that was left to them by an uncle," I reminded him. "Jake had money troubles until that uncle died. It must have been a lot of money."

"Money he probably didn't want to share. Could be Jake killed him and took care of two problems at once," Ethan said with a sigh. "I wish people with family troubles would try to talk things out instead of killing one another."

"It would make life easier for everyone," I said. I looked up and saw Polly heading up the sidewalk in our direction. She smiled and waved at us, and I waved back.

"How are you two doing today?" Polly asked when she got to us.

I smiled. "We're doing all right. The sun has been shining today, and it sure has made me happy."

She nodded. "Isn't it wonderful? It won't be long, and we will be safely out of snowy weather. But I heard on the news that we might get a little more next week."

I groaned. "Don't say that. I'm ready for spring. Actually, I'm ready for summer. I always feel like I never get enough sun."

"You and me both," Polly said with a grin. She turned to Ethan. "Ethan, how are things going? I know it's none of my business, but have you caught the leprechaun killer yet?"

He smiled and shook his head. "No, not yet. I'm still looking into things."

She nodded. "I know that you'll catch the killer soon." She looked over her shoulder and stepped closer to us. "Can I tell you something? It might not be important, but I thought I'd mention it."

Ethan looked at her, squinting, as the sun was setting behind her. "What's that?"

She bit her lower lip and glanced over her shoulder again. "I saw that leprechaun and Andy Hall arguing. Carl and I were there at the pub late one night. The place was full of customers, and when they started shouting, the whole place went silent."

"You saw it yourself?" Ethan asked her.

She nodded. "We were enjoying our dinner when the two of them started arguing. It was awful. Andy accused the leprechaun of stealing."

"Stealing? Stealing what?" Ethan asked.

She shook her head. "We couldn't understand exactly what it was that he thought he had stolen. But they were sure going at it."

"From what I've heard, there was an awful lot of arguing and fighting in that place," I said. "If that keeps up, customers are going to get tired of it and not come in anymore."

She nodded. "Everybody's excited about having a new place to go to eat, and I guess drink if you're a drinker, but nobody wants to have their dinner interrupted by employees of the establishment arguing. Honestly, I don't know if we'll go back."

"It was that bad?" I asked her.

She nodded. "I was shocked and more than a little put off by it."

"They do have excellent food," I pointed out. "And the two times I've been there, I didn't hear any arguing. So maybe this was something that was out of the ordinary that happened."

"That could very well be," she said. "They have really good burgers. Maybe I shouldn't be so quick to judge. I just wanted you to know, Ethan. In case it was important."

Ethan nodded. "You never know. Thanks for the head's up."

She smiled. "I've got to get in there and get some of your mother's fudge, Mia. I know it hasn't been that long since I've been in, but I'm all out, so I'm going to stock up."

"You do that," I said to Polly. "There are a few items that are for St. Patrick's Day, and they'll be gone soon, so you had better get them while you can."

She nodded. "Then I had better hurry up and get inside." She chuckled and headed into the candy store.

I turned and looked at Ethan. "It sure seems like they had an awful lot of trouble down there at the pub. And that's not including the murder."

He nodded. "Sure does. I'll have to stop by and talk to Andy again." He sighed. "Since today is St. Patrick's Day, I better get in there and get some of that mint chocolate chip fudge. I'm going to miss it once it's gone."

"You and me both," I said. He took my hand, and we headed inside the candy store.

We weren't doing anything fancy to celebrate, but I was making corned beef and cabbage for dinner, and hopefully, Ethan would be home early so we could eat together.

Chapter Fifteen

IT WAS TWO DAYS LATER when I headed over to the Pumpkin Hollow Jewelry Store. Nina Black and her husband George owned the jewelry store, and I hoped Nina was working. She helped Ethan pick out a pair of lovely ruby earrings and a ruby tennis bracelet for my Valentine's Day present, and I had intended to stop in and tell her how much I loved them, but I hadn't gotten around to doing it.

"Good morning, Mia. How are you doing?" Nina called from where she stood near a display hanging up necklaces. The Pumpkin Hollow Jewelry Store sold inexpensive touristy items as well as more expensive jewelry.

I smiled as I headed over to her. "I'm doing fine, Nina. I just wanted to stop in and tell you how much I love the ruby earrings and the tennis bracelet that you helped Ethan pick out for me for Valentine's Day." When I got to her, I pulled my hair back so she could see that I was wearing them. "They're so pretty, and I love them so much."

She smiled and nodded. "I'm glad that you like them. After we discussed the jewelry that day you were in here, Ethan stopped by, and I told him that I thought you would enjoy those. I'm so glad I was right."

I nodded. "I love them. I wear them several times a week. I told Ethan that I could probably just leave the earrings in indefinitely, I love them so much."

She chuckled. "It sounds like Ethan needs to get in here and get you some more jewelry, then. A girl needs a variety."

I smiled and looked at the necklaces she was hanging up. They were cute souvenir items that the tourists would go crazy over. "Those are cute."

She nodded. "I'm planning ahead this year. Last year I waited too long to buy stock for Pumpkin Hollow Days, and I didn't order nearly as much as I should have. I love this one." She held out the necklace to me. It was made of orange and white wooden beads, and at the bottom of the necklace was a wooden jack-o'-lantern that grinned.

"It's darling," I said, taking a look at it. "I'll have to get one of those for Pumpkin Hollow Days."

She turned the jack-o'-lantern over. "I had them printed with Pumpkin Hollow Days on the back. I think I'm going to get some more for the Halloween season."

I nodded. "I'm glad you're thinking ahead. I was just thinking the other day that I needed to get some more Halloween printed paper bags ordered for the candy store in the next month or two so that we're prepared."

During the summer we had a two-week event that we called Pumpkin Hollow Days. The Halloween season itself ran from Labor Day weekend until the second weekend in November, and even though it was a lengthy period of time, it just wasn't enough Halloween. People couldn't get enough of Pumpkin Hollow, so we had started Pumpkin Hollow Days. It was a big boost to the town's economy, and it was a lot of fun.

"It will be here before we know it."

She had another box next to her, and I glanced into and saw some green bracelets. "Putting away the St. Patrick's Day items?"

She nodded. "We sold a lot, but not as much as I'd hoped for." She shrugged. "Sometimes you just can't tell. But they'll keep in storage until next St. Patrick's Day, and I won't have to buy as many items next year."

"Thank goodness for that, right?"

She nodded. "Right. Oh, Mia, I heard about that leprechaun getting killed at the pub. Has Ethan found the killer yet?"

I shook my head. "Not yet, but he's working on it. I'm sure he'll arrest the killer any time now."

"I certainly hope so. I hate to hear about him being murdered. Can I tell you something?" she asked, glancing at the one customer that was in the far corner looking at bracelets.

"Yes, what is it?"

She turned back to me and then stepped to the side so that her back was to the customer. "George and I had dinner at the pub the night before the leprechaun was killed. That leprechaun and the owner, Jake Hall, got into an awful argument. It was embarrassing. George and I were some of the last customers to leave that night because we hadn't planned to go out. It was a spur of the moment thing since it was so late when we got around to thinking about having dinner, so we went out that night. They were arguing out in front of the pub. I think they thought all the customers were gone because when they noticed us, I could see that Jake was surprised."

I nodded. How many times had we heard this kind of thing about the people that worked at the pub? "Did you hear what they were arguing about?"

She thought about it a moment. "I heard Jake tell the leprechaun that he had better mind his own business. And then the leprechaun said it was his business, and he was going to say what he had to say about it."

"I wonder what kind of business they were talking about?" I asked, taking this in.

She shook her head. "I didn't hear what the business was that they were talking about, but as we were getting into the car, I heard Jake tell the leprechaun that he was going to regret it. I don't know what it was he was going to regret, but he was angry when he said it."

I gazed at her. "He said it like that? That he was going to regret it?"

She nodded. "Yes, he said it like that. I can't imagine Jake killing anyone, though. You know what I mean? He's always seemed like a nice guy. But I guess they had gotten into some kind of argument, and that was what came out of his mouth. Maybe I should have talked to Ethan about it sooner."

I nodded. "It's hard to say. They were cousins, you know. Maybe it was just a family squabble." *Or maybe Jake had found out about his wife sending love letters to Bubba.*

"Oh. I didn't know that. I bet that's exactly what it was. Sometimes working with family can be tough," she said, glancing at her husband who was sitting at the back counter going over some paperwork. She turned back to me and chuckled. "Not that I would know anything about that kind of thing."

I chuckled. "I know, sometimes family squabbles can get out of hand. I'm thankful that my mom and my sister and I get along fairly well most of the time." It wasn't that Christy and I had never argued, but we had learned to put our differences aside and work together as a team. I couldn't see making one another miserable since we had to see each other at work every day, and the fact that she lived across the street from me meant I couldn't avoid her. Besides that, I loved my sister, and I didn't want to argue with her.

"Well, I hope what I'm saying means absolutely nothing to Ethan and the case. Honestly, I don't want to think of Jake as possibly being the killer. But you know, now that I say that, I completely forgot about something." She got quiet as she thought about it.

"What's that?" I asked.

"I saw that leprechaun and Sabrina Hall at the grocery store several weeks ago. They were having an intense conversation. It wasn't loud or anything, but I could tell that they were really involved in whatever it was they were saying. I didn't realize that he was Jake's cousin though, so maybe it was just something about the pub?"

"Did they seem upset?" I asked.

She hesitated. "Well, I wouldn't exactly say that they were upset. Just very intense. They were whispering to one another, and they seemed very serious."

I nodded. "Maybe they were talking about the pub." Or maybe they were discussing their relationship. I wasn't going to point that out to Nina, but it did make me wonder. And it made me wonder if Jake had found out that they were having a relationship. But then, we didn't know for sure if they really were having a relationship. Maybe the letters were just Sabrina's fantasy, and because he was coming to California, she thought they might be able to begin a relationship. Because when he was in Ohio, how on earth would they have been able to carry on a relationship other than by letters and phone calls?

She shrugged and hung up the necklace. "I meant to get into the candy store and get some of that fudge that your mom made for St. Patrick's Day. I had several customers come in here and tell me how good it was, and I told George I was going to stop by, but I didn't make it. I don't suppose she's still making it?"

I shook my head. "No, sorry. Mom is a stickler for her holidays and the types of candy that she makes. She won't be making any more of it for a while. But I'm sure she'll have a new flavor made for spring. Maybe even something different for Easter."

"Well, you can bet I'm not going to miss out on any of that," Nina said.

I picked up the wooden Pumpkin Hollow Days necklace she had just hung up. "You know what? I think I'm going to buy this. It's really cute." Each of the beads was textured and beveled, and the little jack-o'-lantern was as cute as could be. If I didn't get it now, it would probably sell out quickly.

She nodded. "I was thinking I need to get one for myself. Come on, I'll ring you up."

I followed her over to the cash register to pay for the necklace. It would be adorable to wear for both Pumpkin Hollow Days and the Halloween season.

Chapter Sixteen

WHAT NINA SAID ABOUT Bubba and Jake arguing the night before he died made me wonder. Had Jake told Bubba that he was going to fire him? If he had, why was Bubba at the pub the next day? Maybe Jake had threatened to fire him, and that was what the argument was about.

The next evening Ethan had the chance to leave work early. It was just after 4:30 and early for dinner, but we decided to call an order in to the pub and stop by to pick it up and eat it at home. When we walked into the pub, there weren't many customers there. A couple of employees were busy making sure everything was ready for the night's service, and the kitchen door was open. We went up to the cash register to see if our meals were ready.

"I'm starving," Ethan said. "I didn't get a chance to eat lunch until two o'clock, and since I knew I was going to be able to leave early today, I decided to wait."

"Then you must be starving," I said. "I couldn't go that long without eating anything."

"I could eat a horse," he said.

Jake came out of the back room, and when he saw us, he nodded and headed over to us. "Hello Ethan, hello Mia. How are you two this afternoon?"

"We're doing great," I said. "We called in an order, and we're hoping that it's ready."

He nodded. "You have the call in order? The two burgers?"

I smiled. "Those are the ones."

"I think it's going to be just a couple more minutes." He glanced at Ethan. "Ethan, how is that murder investigation going?"

Ethan stepped closer to the counter. "It's going all right, I guess. Jake, I heard a rumor, and I wondered if you could tell me whether it was true or not."

Jake's eyes widened slightly, and he nodded. "Sure. What is it?"

"I heard you were going to fire Bubba. Is that true?"

Jake's eyes went wider as he stared at Ethan. Then he frowned and nodded. "It's true. I mean, it's not true that I did fire him, but I was thinking about it. We were close when we were kids, but Bubba had changed over the years. Once I got him here to California and put him to work, I realized that he really didn't like working. He was lazy, and he kept ordering all the employees around. You wouldn't believe the complaints I got about him from the other employees."

"Did you say something to him about it?" Ethan asked.

He nodded. "I told him several times that if there was an issue with the employees to let me handle it. But it was like it went in one ear and out the other. He just kept sticking his nose into things that didn't concern him."

"So did you threaten to fire him?" I asked him.

He hesitated and didn't make eye contact. "We argued. I told him that if he didn't straighten up, I was going have to let him go."

"What did he say to that?" Ethan asked.

He sighed. "He got angry. He threatened me. Told me I was going to be sorry if I did something like that."

"What did you say to that?" Ethan asked.

He shrugged. "What could I say? I told him that I was the boss, and he wasn't going to threaten me. I was going to run my business the way I saw fit, and if he didn't like it, then he could go back to Ohio."

"And how did he feel about that?" I asked.

He shook his head and shrugged again. "He yelled some obscenities at me, and I went home. With Bubba, it was best just to let him cool off after he got heated up. No use in continuing the argument with him. He wasn't going to quit."

"I heard the two of you got into an argument here at the pub," I said carefully. I didn't look at Ethan when I said it. I didn't know how he would feel about me asking the question. "Someone said the two of you got into an argument about your uncle. Something about a will."

His mouth made a straight line, and his brow furrowed. "Yeah, I bet I know who told you that. It was Marissa, wasn't it?"

I shrugged. "Honestly, I don't remember who told me that." It was a lie, and I knew that he knew that. But I wasn't going to name names.

"Yeah, I know it was her. Yes, we got into an argument about it. She was here in the pub, so I know she's the one who told you.

It was a stupid argument. Our uncle left us both some money, and Bubba swore that he left me more than he did him. But the thing is, Bubba was terrible with money, and he blew everything he was given. That isn't my fault. He needed to be more careful with his money."

"Is it true that you got more money than he did?" Ethan asked.

He hesitated. "To be honest, I'm not sure if it's true or not. I know how much money our uncle left me. And Bubba claimed that he only left him $10,000, which is a lot less than what I was given. But I think Bubba was lying about it. He liked to gamble, and he liked to blow his money. He was always like that. When we were teenagers, he'd spend his allowance within an hour of having gotten it while I hung onto mine. And then he was always bumming money off me for a soda or baseball cards or whatever it was that he wanted. He was just terrible with money."

"So you think he was lying about how much money he got?" I asked carefully. From all that I'd heard about Bubba, it wouldn't surprise me if he had lied.

He nodded. "Yes, I think he lied, and he hoped I would give him some of my money, just like in the old days."

"That takes gumption," Ethan said.

He nodded. "Sure does. But let me tell you about Marissa." He looked over his shoulder to make sure no one was near enough to overhear him, then turned back to us. "She had a thing for Bubba. I really can't understand why. I mean, Bubba was funny, and some girls like that, so maybe that was the attraction. And it was Bubba that got Marissa the job with us here. I had a couple of other applicants that I thought would be better, but Bubba insisted that we hire her. Turns out Marissa is just as controlling as Bubba was. She couldn't stand it whenever another woman would look in Bubba's direction."

"Is it true that she was cleaning your house before she came to work here at the pub?" I asked him.

He nodded. "Yeah, Bubba insisted that we put her to work before there was anything here for her to do. I told him there wasn't any way I was going to do that. If she wanted a job, she was going to have to wait a few more weeks. But then my wife suggested that we could hire her to do the housework at home. We had been so busy that we were neglecting a lot of things around the house. After we'd worked here all day, we weren't in the mood to go home and clean."

Sabrina had told us this, but I wondered if Jake had something more to tell us about Marissa.

"And you trusted her enough to leave her alone in your house?" Ethan asked.

He shrugged. "My wife trusted her enough. I don't know if it was a wise decision, but she did. Now that I know Marissa a little better, I'm not sure I would have agreed to allow her to be in the house by herself."

"And why is that?" Ethan asked.

He shrugged. "I'm just saying that she's always causing trouble. She was jealous of Bubba, and she causes trouble with the other waitresses and barmaids. It's like she's not happy unless she's stirring something up. People like that always make me wonder what else they might be up to. There's something about a person that needs to cause trouble all the time that makes me not trust them."

I couldn't argue with Jake. I'd worked with a couple of people like that in the past, and I couldn't say that he was wrong.

"Jake, what happened to Bubba's belongings after he died? He was living with you and your wife, wasn't he?" Ethan asked him.

He nodded. "Yeah, my wife packed everything up, and we shipped the important things off to his mother. Why?"

Ethan shrugged and glanced at me. "I just wondered. There wasn't anything in his personal belongings that might have been of interest? Maybe something that might have hinted at what might have happened to him?"

He shook his head. "If there was, Sabrina didn't mention it. I can ask her."

He nodded. "Sure. Maybe ask her if there was anything she saw."

We turned as Marissa brought up our to-go order and set it on the counter. "Hello Mia, hello Ethan. Here's your dinner."

"Thanks, Marissa," Ethan said.

Ethan paid for our food, and we said goodbye and headed out to Ethan's truck. When we got inside, I turned and looked at him. "Couldn't you have served them with a search warrant for their house?"

He shook his head. "A judge would want some kind of proof that it was necessary. Bubba was killed here at the pub, and we had no reason to think that the killer would have left some kind of evidence in his room. But I sure would like to know if those letters exist or not."

"You and me both," I agreed. If Sabrina had cleared out his room, it was a cinch that she had those letters and we would never see them.

Chapter Seventeen

"I MISSED YOU TODAY," I said, squeezing Ethan tight. Boo and Licorice wrapped themselves around our legs as we stood there in the living room. The day had turned chilly, and he had started a fire in the fireplace as soon as he had gotten home. I was looking forward to a quiet, romantic evening with just the two of us. Had I known he was going to get off early again, I would have made a romantic dinner, but as it was, I ordered pizza for us.

He chuckled, burying his face in my hair. "I missed you more," he murmured in my ear.

I grinned, and before I could say anything else, there was a knock at the door, and then it swung open. I groaned.

"Hey, what are you two doing?" Christy asked, walking through the door without waiting for an invitation. Devon followed behind her.

"Oh, we aren't interrupting anything, are we?" Devon asked when he saw Ethan with his arms around me.

Ethan released me, and I looked at Christy, narrowing my eyes at her. "No Devon, you aren't interrupting anything." Ethan went over and sat on the couch.

"Oh good," Christy said. She walked to the middle of the living room and then stopped, sniffing the air. "Wait a minute. I don't smell anything."

"What were you expecting to smell?" I asked.

"Dinner." She turned and looked at me. "What are we having for dinner?"

I sighed and rolled my eyes. "Pizza. It just hasn't been delivered yet."

"Oh," she said disappointedly. "But that's okay. I like pizza. I was just hoping you were going to make us a gourmet meal. I've been bragging to Devon about your cooking skills. It's a shame he won't get to try something you made this evening."

I turned and looked at Devon as he crouched down to pet Boo and Licorice. "Sorry, Devon, you're going to be disappointed."

He looked up at me and grinned. "Are you kidding? Pizza never disappoints me. Sorry for barging in on you like that."

I shook my head and went to sit next to Ethan. "Don't worry about it. We're getting used to it." I looked at Christy pointedly.

She chuckled and headed into the kitchen. "I hope you've got some iced tea in here."

"When do I not have iced tea in the refrigerator?" I asked.

"That's what I thought. Anyone else want any?" she called from the kitchen. I heard the refrigerator door open and then shut.

"I'd love some iced tea," Devon said and came over and sat on the loveseat across from us. "Really, we don't have to stay. Christy just thought we'd stop by and say hello and see what you were doing."

"If I know my sister, she was coming over here for dinner," I said. "It's okay, though. Honestly, we were just going to eat pizza and maybe watch a little television."

"We live exciting lives around here, Devon," Ethan said.

Devon chuckled, and Boo jumped in his lap.

"Here we are," Christy said, coming back into the living room and handing a glass of iced tea to Devon. "Sweetened just like you like it."

"Thanks, babe," he said, taking it from her.

Christy sat down next to him and turned to Ethan. "Okay, Ethan, spill it. What's going on with the leprechaun case?"

"Christy, there's absolutely nothing going on with the case. In fact, we decided that because it was only a leprechaun that was murdered, it doesn't really matter, and we're just moving on."

Christy narrowed her eyes at him. "Telling lies will make your nose grow."

He shrugged. "I guess I'll have to take the chance."

The doorbell rang. "Thank goodness, I'm starving," I said.

Ethan answered the door and paid for the pizza, and we all headed into the kitchen. Fortunately, we had bought an extra-large so that we would have leftovers. With Christy and Devon joining us, we weren't going to have those leftovers, but that was fine. It would just give us an excuse to buy another pizza in a couple of days.

Christy opened the pizza box while I got some plates and napkins and put them on the table. "Hawaiian pizza? What were you two thinking?"

"We were thinking that we love Hawaiian pizza," I informed her and sat down next to Ethan. "You can eat it, or you can just watch us eat it. Your choice."

She chuckled. "I'm certainly not going to sit here and watch you all eat. It smells great, and I like Hawaiian pizza anyway."

We all served ourselves, and for the next few minutes, there wasn't much conversation as we dug into the pizza. After I finished my slice, I turned to Ethan. "So what is really going on with the leprechaun murder?"

He shrugged and took another bite of his pizza. I reached for another slice.

"I'm working on it. You know how it is."

I nodded. "I do know how it is." I got up and poured a glass of tea for myself and Ethan, and sat back down.

"What happened at the pub was kind of crazy. I still can't believe that the leprechaun was killed," Devon said as he helped himself to another slice of pizza.

Ethan nodded. "Never did I think that I was going to be investigating the murder of a leprechaun."

Devon chuckled, and then he was quiet for a moment. "You know what? I heard something that might be considered just a rumor, but my friend Rick works part-time down there as a dishwasher. He only gets about fifteen or twenty hours a week because it's a side job. But he said Andy Hall and the leprechaun didn't like each other."

"I've heard that," Ethan said noncommittally. "It seems to be going around town."

Devon nodded. "Yeah, I guess it is. But he said he overheard a conversation between Andy Hall and his dad, Jake. Andy wanted his father to fire the leprechaun."

We had heard this before, but suddenly my Spidey senses were tingling. "Exactly what did he say?"

Devon turned to me. "Andy and his dad got into an argument. His dad said he couldn't fire him because he was his cousin, but Andy kept pressuring him. Andy said that the leprechaun was ruining their business, and he had to fire him."

"And what did Jake say to that?" Ethan asked.

"Jake said he would talk to him. And that's when he said Andy blew a gasket. He told his dad that talking to him wasn't going to do any good. He said he had already talked to him, and Bubba didn't care about anything that was said to him. He told his dad that he had no choice but to fire him. But Jake didn't want to do that. He said he wasn't going to do it. And that was when they got into a real fight. They were behind closed doors, but I guess the walls are thin in the office back there, and the two of them were screaming at one another."

"Screaming? Did he say they were actually screaming?" I asked.

He nodded. "He said he had never seen people act that way on the job. He said he's looking for another job because he just can't take all the arguing that goes on there."

"What else did Andy say?" Christy asked him.

"He said that if Jake didn't handle the situation, he would handle it himself. And that was when Jake started threatening

Andy. He told him he better keep his nose out of his business, and he didn't have any right to decide how he was going to run his business."

"That sounds crazy," I said.

"Yeah, why couldn't they just have a civilized conversation?" Christy asked.

Devon shrugged. "It seems like there's a lot of hotheaded people there at the pub. At least according to Rick. But the thing that really caught Rick's attention was when Andy told his father that he was going to handle things. He couldn't believe it."

"Maybe Andy handled things by killing the leprechaun," Christy pointed out.

Ethan took another bite of his pizza, thinking about this. "Maybe. Or maybe it was just the way they were with each other. Arguing all the time. I hate to think that Andy had anything to do with the leprechaun's death."

I didn't blame Ethan. I would feel bad if Andy killed his father's cousin. He seemed like a good guy, and I couldn't picture him killing anyone.

Chapter Eighteen

"SO WHAT DO YOU THINK?" Christy asked, turning to me. "Who killed our little green friend?"

I turned to her as we sat at a table at Amanda's coffee shop again. The weather was still brisk out, and hot coffee was all I was interested in today. "Marissa Fields. She killed the leprechaun."

Christy sat back in her chair, thinking about it. "Why? Why would she do something like that? She's a cute, sweet girl that comes from a good family. Why would she kill?"

I took a sip of my vanilla mummy latte. "Because she was desperate to get married, and apparently she would latch onto any available man. And the leprechaun was available, and you know he was flattered by somebody like Marissa taking an interest in him. But the problem was, he had eyes for other women, and that made Marissa jealous."

She nodded and took a sip of her coffee. There were several other customers in the shop, and we were in the back corner discussing the case. Amanda was busy making coffee, but occasionally she would glance back in our direction. I knew she wanted to take a break and hang out with us, but she was busy. The baby was in a baby carrier she wore on her chest and was sleeping. If she hadn't been asleep, I would have taken her from her mother so I could visit with her.

"I think you're right. Marissa is our killer. There's just something about her that says she's going to get what she wants no matter the cost."

"I agree. I mean, Marissa should have gone to college right after high school, but instead, she's working these part-time jobs. I really think it's because her parents are probably still paying a lot of her bills, and she doesn't need to take responsibility for her life." It wasn't that I knew her well enough to come to this conclusion, it just seemed odd to me that she wasn't doing something more productive with her life.

She took another sip of her coffee. "When you work jobs at restaurants or bars, you're going to meet a lot of guys. A lot of available guys. Maybe it's true that all she wanted was to get married."

I nodded and took a bite of the blueberry muffin I had gotten to go with my coffee. "Unfortunately, you're also going to run into a lot of guys that aren't available, but some women don't care about that."

"Did you tell Ethan that you thought it was Marissa?"

I nodded. "Yes, I never keep my opinions to myself about this kind of thing."

"And what does he think?"

"You know how he is. He won't commit to anything until he's made the arrest. Or at least, he won't commit to telling me who he believes the killer is."

She took a sip of her coffee. "So what are we going to do about it? What if Ethan doesn't arrest her, and she goes on and lives her life any way she wants? What if she kills another man? She's the jealous type, and if she gets away with it once, you know she's going to do it again."

I chuckled. "Easy, there, sister. We'll have to wait and let Ethan do his job. He'll arrest her. I'm sure of it."

We looked up, and I was surprised to see Marissa walk through the coffee shop door and get in line. I turned and looked at Christy, and she nodded at me.

"There's our suspect now. I just can't imagine killing someone like that. Especially slashing their throat. When you slash someone's throat, you've got to get up close and personal with your victim, and you've got to really not care about them," Christy whispered.

I took another sip of my coffee. "I don't know that she didn't care about him. I think she cared too much about him. And knowing that he was flirting with other women enraged her. She killed him in a fit of rage." I was sure I was right about this. She would have killed him and then slipped back into the employee restroom at the pub, cleaned herself up, and disposed of the apron. How easy would it have been for her to head back into the kitchen and pick up a new apron? It was so busy that night that no one would have noticed her picking up another apron and putting it on. And if they did, they wouldn't think to question her about where the apron that she had been wearing was.

We watched the line at the counter dwindle down, and finally, Amanda waited on Marissa.

I turned and looked at Christy. "I wish Ethan would get on with it and arrest her," I whispered.

Christy nodded vigorously. "He needs to do it. You need to give him a call and let him know that she's here so he can come down here and arrest her."

"I'm sure he knows where she's at. And when he gets ready to arrest her, he'll do it."

She shook her head. "Maybe she's been hiding from him? Maybe he's out on the street looking for her right now."

I smirked. "I'm pretty sure that she wouldn't come here to hide, especially since the wife of the detective on the case is here."

"But she didn't know that when she came in here," Christy insisted.

"But she would have left when she saw me," I whispered.

She sighed. "All right, fine. I guess you've got a point."

When Marissa had paid for her coffee, she headed in our direction. She definitely wasn't hiding from anyone. She was coming to talk to us.

She smiled when she got to us. "Good morning, Mia, good morning, Christy. How are you girls doing today?"

"We're doing great," I said as Christy sat back in her seat, her eyes riveted to Marissa.

"It's so cold out there this morning. I had to pick up a large latte." She held the cup up to show us.

I nodded. "That's the same reason we're here."

Amanda came up behind her and sat down across from me. "Wow, that was a nice little morning rush. I've got to get off my feet for a minute. The extra weight of this baby makes my feet hurt."

I looked at the baby and smiled. "She's so sweet."

"So Marissa, how are things going?" Christy asked. "How have you been, knowing that a murder occurred at your workplace?"

Marissa's eyes widened slightly. "Well, nobody's happy about that, you know, but we're doing our best to cope with it."

"I bet you're coping with it," Christy said, narrowing her eyes at her. "I bet you're coping with the fact that you killed that poor leprechaun."

Marissa gasped, and I kicked Christy under the table.

"I did no such thing! What are you talking about?"

"Everyone knows that you're jealous," Christy said. "Why don't you just admit that you got jealous because the leprechaun was flirting with everyone he ran into, and you got mad, and you killed him."

I glanced at Amanda. Her mouth was open as she watched the conversation like she was following a tennis match.

Marissa narrowed her eyes at Christy. "You're out of your mind. I did no such thing. And besides that, everybody in the kitchen knows that I was there. I have plenty of alibis."

"Do you?" Christy asked. "Because I think it would have been pretty easy to slip back into the restroom and get cleaned up and then get back to work without anybody knowing anything. The pub was so busy that night that there's no way anybody had time to make sure you were doing your job and not out back killing someone."

I could see Marissa's hand tightening on her coffee cup, and her face turned pink. "Christy Jordan, you are out of your mind. You can ask the cook. We were so busy that I was there helping him make salads all evening long. Everyone knows that. Even Ethan knows that."

Oh. If Ethan knew this, then he failed to mention it to me. "Does he?" I asked.

She turned and glared at me. "I told him that. I told him exactly what I was doing that evening."

Now we were in trouble. Christy had accused a possible murder suspect, and Ethan wasn't going to be happy about that.

"I don't believe you," Christy insisted. "It was so busy that night that nobody would have had time to keep an eye on you. Just because you made a few salads for the cook doesn't mean that you did it all evening long. Does it?"

She breathed out hard and pinned Christy with a glare. "You don't know what you're talking about. I was making salads all evening long." With that, she spun around and left the coffee shop.

I turned and looked at Christy. "Good going. You know Ethan's going to get angry at us if she tells him what you just did."

She shrugged. "You know what I said was true. Nobody kept an eye on her all that time, making sure that she was working. She had plenty of time to slip out there and kill Bubba. And she isn't going to tell Ethan because she doesn't want him to take a closer look at her."

"She may have had time to go out back and kill him," Amanda said and took a sip of her coffee. "But accusing her isn't going to get her to admit to it. She's going to cling to her story as long as she can."

Amanda had a point. There was no way she was going to back down from her story. But maybe she would let something slip and Ethan could arrest her.

Chapter Nineteen

"WHAT ARE YOU DOING, Christy?" I asked as she sealed a tin of fudge. We had already finished packing up all the Internet orders for the day.

She looked at me and grinned. "Peanut butter fudge." She held up the tin.

I nodded. "Yes, that's peanut butter fudge. What are you doing with it?"

"I've been thinking about things, and I decided that we need to stop by and pay a visit to Sabrina Hall."

I frowned. "And why would we do that?"

She leaned in close to me to whisper. "I think she's got to be our killer. If Marissa isn't the killer, then Sabrina is."

I considered this for a moment. "Because of the love letters?"

She nodded. "Because of the love letters."

"We don't know if those love letters actually exist. Marissa said she found them, but we've never seen them. What if she was lying? You know how jealous she is. She might have made it up to frame Sabrina."

She nodded. "Maybe the letters exist, maybe they don't. Why don't we go and see if we can find out?"

"I don't trust you. You're going to accuse her of murder, and we're going to get in trouble." I had explained to Ethan what happened with Marissa at the coffee shop as gently as I could, and he had been very unhappy. Thankfully, I hadn't mentioned it until after Christy and Devon stopped by for dinner again because he might've thrown her out on her ear.

She held up two fingers. "Scout's honor, I will not accuse Sabrina of murder."

I narrowed my eyes at her. "You were never a scout."

"So? That doesn't mean that I can't swear that I won't do it. Come on. Let's go talk to her."

I nodded and turned to Linda. "Linda, we're going to go home now. We'll see you in the morning."

"See you girls later," Linda said. "Have a good evening."

"Thanks," Christy said as we headed out to my car.

WHEN WE PULLED UP TO the Hall's house, Sabrina was walking out the door with a cardboard box in her hands. Andy was following behind her with another box.

"I wonder what they're doing?" Christy asked, tilting her head.

I shook my head and opened my car door. "Let's go find out."

We got out of my car and headed over to where they were standing near their car. The trunk was open, and Andy put his box inside, his eyes never leaving us.

"Hello, Andy. Hello, Sabrina," I said. "How are you both doing this evening?"

Sabrina looked at the cloudy sky and then turned back to me and smiled. "We're doing just fine, as long as it doesn't start raining. But I'm afraid the skies may open up any moment." She set the box in the trunk. If I wasn't mistaken, there was a slight edge to her voice.

"What are you two up to?" Andy asked us, then glanced at his mother.

"We thought we'd stop by and see how you all were doing," Christy answered. "And since we just got off work, we thought we'd bring you a tin of peanut butter fudge. I hope you like peanut butter."

Andy nodded. "Sure, we like peanut butter."

"That's sweet of you to bring us some fudge," Sabrina said with a nod. She smiled, but it seemed forced.

"I'm so glad you like peanut butter fudge. It didn't even occur to me until we were almost here that you might have a peanut allergy." Christy chuckled and shook her head. "Leave it to me to not even think about that."

"No. No peanut allergies here," Sabrina said. I moved closer to the trunk of their car, and I was just able to see that there were several more cardboard boxes in the trunk before Andy slammed it shut. Sabrina put her hands in her coat pockets. "That's nice of you to bring it by. We were just on our way to the new rummage shop. We have a bunch of things that we wanted to get rid of."

"Oh? I like that place. I've been in there a couple of times, and it's nice that the proceeds support the local animal shelter," I said.

Sabrina nodded. "It also helps pay for the spay and neuter of stray dogs and cats."

"That's a great idea," Christy said, still holding the tin of fudge. If I wasn't mistaken, Sabrina and Andy seemed a bit nervous now.

"Well, we had better get going," Andy said, but he didn't make a move.

Christy held out the tin of fudge to Sabrina. "Well, here you are. We just wondered how you all were doing with the loss of Cousin Bubba."

She smiled and glanced at Andy. "That's kind of you to think of us, and Jake is taking it hard, of course. He's out of town right now. He flew to Ohio to attend the funeral."

"He mentioned he was going to do that," I said, leaning on the car. "It's a shame that the two of you couldn't go with him. I'm sure he would've appreciated the support."

Sabrina gave me a surprised look while Andy jingled the keys in his pocket. "We wanted to go with him, but the airline prices were so expensive. We've already put so much money into the pub and the new house that we just couldn't afford two more tickets. But he's got his aunt and uncle and a handful of cousins to visit with while he's there," she said.

I nodded. "Thank goodness he won't be on his own completely."

She glanced at Andy. "Well, that was kind of you to think of us. Thank you for bringing us the fudge. We had better get going."

"What kind of things are you donating?" Christy asked.

Andy narrowed his eyes at her but didn't say anything.

Sabrina sighed. "Oh, just some old clothes and books that we boxed up."

"Bubba's old clothes and books?" I asked.

She hesitated. "Well, there were a few of his things in there. It's not like we could hold on to them forever."

"And letters?" Christy asked. "Were there some letters among his things?"

Sabrina's eyes went wide, and she shook her head slowly. "What are you talking about?"

"We've got to get going," Andy said gruffly. "If you two will excuse us."

He headed for the driver's side door, but his mother stood there staring at us.

"Letters," Christy said. "Maybe some love letters?"

She narrowed her eyes at Christy. "I don't know what you're talking about. Why would Bubba have love letters?"

Andy opened the car door. "Mom, let's get going. It's going to start raining any minute now."

Sabrina nodded. "We've got to get going. The sky is going to open up any moment, and we're going to be stuck in the middle of a downpour. Thank you so much for the fudge." She went around us to get to the passenger side door.

"Then what about the love letters?" Christy asked.

Sabrina shook her head without looking at her. "I have no idea what you're talking about."

Andy glared at Christy over the top of the car. Christy met his gaze, and then she smiled. "Andy, you know about the letters, don't you?"

He shook his head. "I have no idea what you're talking about."

"Of course you do. That's why you were so insistent that your father fire Bubba. Because you knew about the love letters."

Andy gritted his teeth and slammed the car door shut. He came around the side of the car, and Christy and I ran for my car.

"I'll kill you!" Andy seethed.

Fortunately for me, I hadn't put my car keys away, and we jumped in my car and locked the doors as he pounded on the window on the passenger side. Christy screamed, and I started the car and pulled away.

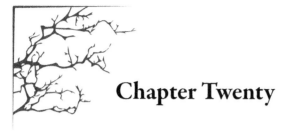

Chapter Twenty

IT WAS LATE WHEN ETHAN got home that night. I was sitting on the couch, a fire in the fireplace. I looked up at him as he walked through the door. He stopped and looked at me.

"Are you hungry?" I asked him.

He nodded. "I'm starving."

I glanced at the clock on the wall. It was just after midnight. "I made chicken and dumplings. Let me heat some up for you."

I put some chicken and dumplings into a bowl and put it into the microwave to warm up. "I also made you a peach cobbler."

"Really? All of that for me?"

I turned and smiled at him. "I thought I might need to make it up to you."

"Your sister needs to make it up to me."

"Yeah, probably so. Christy needs to keep her mouth shut. But you've got to hand it to her. She was right this time."

He snorted. "This time. What about all the other times?"

I grinned. "She'll never let you live it down. You know how she is."

He sat down at the kitchen table and sighed. "Where are the cats?"

"They're in bed," I said. "They got tired of waiting for you. So, what did they say?"

The front door swung open. "Wait a minute! I need in on all of this," Christy called, hurrying into the kitchen.

I turned and looked at him. "You need to remember to lock the door behind yourself."

He nodded. "Apparently so. Christy, I'm not happy with you."

She smiled and sat down in the chair across from him. "Mia, can I have some chicken and dumplings?"

"You had some for dinner," I said. We had eaten chicken and dumplings for dinner.

"I'm starving," she said, pleading with me.

I nodded and filled another bowl with chicken and dumplings for her, and then one for me. It tasted too good not to have another bowl.

Christy leaned over the table. "So, go on Ethan, what happened?"

He stared at her steadily. "You already know what happened."

She shook her head. "No, we were just guessing at what happened. Sabrina and Andy killed Bubba?"

He was quiet for a minute. "Andy killed Bubba. He found his mother's letters in Bubba's room, and he knew that if he didn't get rid of Bubba, he and his mother were going to have an affair. He couldn't bear the thought of her cheating on his father, so he killed Bubba."

"That's awful," I said and set the bowl of soup in front of him.

"This smells good," he said and took a bite, nodding. "Excellent."

"Thanks," I said and put another bowl of chicken and dumplings into the microwave. "So Sabrina didn't have anything to do with his murder?"

"She didn't have anything to do with the actual murder, but she did have something to do with covering it up. She knew what Andy had done, and she confronted him. He denied it at first, but then eventually he conceded that he had done it. She was brokenhearted, of course. She thought she was in love. But she couldn't stand to see her only son go to prison, so she hid the evidence."

"What evidence?" I asked.

"His bloody clothes. He came home and took his clothes off and took a shower, and he was going to put them into the dumpster. But Sabrina was afraid somebody would go digging through the trash and find them, so she helped him bury them in the backyard."

"And were they back there?" I asked. I took the bowl of soup out of the microwave and put it in front of Christy.

"Thanks, Mia," she said and picked up the spoon.

He nodded. "Yes, they were buried out behind their potting shed."

"So Sabrina brought up the idea that Marissa could have put her bloody apron in the garbage can at work to throw us off," I said.

He nodded. "She was hoping to pin the murder on her."

I sighed. "That's just a shame."

He nodded. "The things people do in the name of love."

"The things people do in the name of murder," Christy corrected.

"That too," he said, nodding. "If they just handled things like adults, Andy wouldn't be looking at spending a long time in prison. Maybe the rest of his life."

"What about Sabrina? Is she going to prison?" I asked.

He nodded. "Most likely. But she won't spend as much time in jail as Andy will."

"So did Sabrina really have an affair with Bubba?" Christy asked.

He shrugged. "She swears that she didn't. She said she wanted to, but that he was interested in Marissa. I don't know if she's telling the truth or if we'll ever really know."

"That's just sad," I said. "Honestly, why can't people just behave themselves?"

He chuckled. "It sure would make things easier, wouldn't it?"

I nodded and removed my bowl from the microwave, and sat next to Ethan. "I'm just glad that you caught the killer."

"Jake must be devastated," Christy said. "He lost three family members this month." Boo and Licorice wandered into the kitchen, having smelled the chicken and dumplings warming up. "Well, there's the Bobbsey twins."

"They were sleeping," I said. Boo rubbed up against my legs. I wasn't fooled. He didn't want attention; he wanted some chicken and dumplings.

"It's a shame that poor Jake is going to have to go without having his family around," Ethan said.

I nodded. "I agree. It is a shame."

"So Jake didn't know anything about what Andy and Sabrina were up to?" Christy asked.

He shook his head. "Not a thing. Poor guy thought some stranger killed his cousin."

It really was a shame that Jake was going to have to deal with his son murdering his cousin and his wife wanting to have an affair with him. I was glad the leprechaun killer had been found, but I was sad about who it was.

The End

Sign up for my newsletter to receive updates on new releases and deals

https://www.subscribepage.com/kathleen-suzette

Follow me on Facebook:

https://www.facebook.com/
Kathleen-Suzette-Kate-Bell-authors-759206390932120/

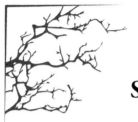

Sneak Peek

Wedding Bell Blunders
    A Freshly Baked Cozy Mystery, book 11
Chapter One

"Oh!" I squealed as I ducked my head and ran inside the house. The rain was dripping off the eaves and my knit hat got soaked as I crossed beneath it. My arms were filled with cardboard boxes. There was a larger box at the bottom, and three smaller ones were stacked on top of it, and I balanced them so they didn't topple off. I stopped and looked around the empty house. The sound of the rain on the roof was hypnotic.

"We had better hurry and get this done before we get soaked," Alec said, coming up behind me. "Why don't we just set all the boxes in the ballroom for now? Then you can go through them and decide where it all goes."

I nodded and followed him into the ballroom. We set our boxes down in the middle of the room.

"Isn't this lovely?" I asked, looking around the ballroom. The old Jensen mansion was coming together nicely.

Alec and I had bought the house late last year when the body of a woman that had been missing for ten years had been found in the bathtub upstairs. Turns out you can get a house for a steal when a dead body is found there. The first question everyone asked when they found out that we had bought the mansion is, aren't you afraid of ghosts? The answer is, no. I don't believe in them.

We'd had workers come in and restore some of the original woodwork that had been painted over, as well as do some repairs to the house. Alec and I had decided to wait to move in until most of the larger projects were finished.

He nodded and glanced around. "It is nice. Can't you just picture the Christmas tree placed up against those windows," he said, pointing to the French doors.

"We can't put it right up against them. We won't be able to use the French doors if we do that."

He shrugged. "Why do you want to use the French doors in the wintertime? I can see that we'll need to use them during the summer to go outside to barbecue, but when it's snowing, we don't need to use those doors."

I shook my head. "No, we're going to get the biggest Christmas tree we can find, and we're going to put it in the middle of this room. It will be the centerpiece. We need to be able to use the French doors to go outside and build snowmen when we have grandchildren." I was looking ahead. My kids weren't even married yet. Alec had been married once, but he had never had children, so my future grandchildren were also going to be his.

He chuckled. "All right, whatever you say. Let's go get the rest of the boxes."

We headed back out into the rain. Alec's SUV was filled with boxes from my house. We were finally doing it. We were moving into our new house. Or rather, I was moving into our new house. I'm an old-fashioned girl, and I told Alec that I wasn't going to live with him before marriage, and I meant it.

Packing up my old house was sad. My husband, Thaddeus, had been gone for a long time now, but every corner of that house reminded me of him. As I was packing things up, the memories overtook me. Everything we had done, everything we had said to one another. Everything. My kids had been born in that house, and now I was leaving it behind. I swallowed back the lump that was forming with the memories and I grabbed two more cardboard boxes and hurried with them inside the house, slipping on the hardwood floor. "Whoa!"

Alec chuckled. "Are you all right?"

"I'm all right," I said as I regained my footing and headed to the ballroom, placing these boxes with the others.

"You better be careful on these wet floors. We should have brought a throw rug to put in front of the door. I didn't even think about it."

I nodded. "I didn't think about it either. It will be all right. We'll just be careful."

"So what do you think? When do I get to move in here?" He looked at me, one eyebrow raised.

I smiled. "After I get moved in."

I headed back out to the SUV to get more boxes.

"Really? You're going to let me move in with you?" he asked, coming up behind me.

I chuckled and shook my head. "No. Or at least, not until we get married."

He groaned and rolled his eyes. "Okay then, when do we get married?" He picked up a big box that I knew was filled with books, and he grunted. "What did you do, pack all the bricks from the backyard?"

I shook my head. "Don't be silly. Those are just books."

He snorted. "Don't you believe in ereaders?" He hefted the box, groaning, and headed toward the house.

"Of course I believe in ereaders, But I still love my physical books." I picked up two lighter boxes and followed behind him. "Don't you miss the smell of books?"

He nodded. "Sometimes. I miss going into brick-and-mortar bookstores too. Maybe when we get moved, we should take a drive by the one over in Bangor and spend a couple of hours looking through the stacks."

"That's a great idea," I said. "Especially with this cold, rainy weather, it would be fun to bring some books back here and read in front of the fire."

He nodded, and we headed into the ballroom and set the boxes down with the others. He straightened up.

"Seriously, Allie, when are we getting married?" he looked at me, eyebrow raised again.

I took a deep breath. And then I looked at the weather outside the French doors. The rain was coming down harder, and it was freezing cold. We had discussed having a beach wedding, and that was what I had in mind. But it was the end of March, and I knew we weren't going to have real beach weather for a couple more months. If we were lucky, we would have it at the beginning of May, but May weather on the coast of Maine could be tricky. One day you'd have a pretty day, and the next day it would look like it did it today. I turned to him. "I don't know. I thought we were going to have a beach wedding?"

He shrugged. "Does it really matter? I don't care if we have a beach wedding, or if we just go down to City Hall and get married there."

"Really? You would get married at City Hall?"

He nodded. "Sure. Why not? We've been married before, and you said you didn't want the big white wedding dress and the fancy formal sit-down dinner. So why not go to City Hall and get married in front of the justice of the peace?"

I sighed. "No, I don't need a great big wedding. But I think getting married at City Hall is going to be a little disappointing for me."

He nodded. "I figured as much. So what do you want to do? And why do we have to wait? We don't need the beach wedding."

I nodded and then turned and headed back to get more boxes from the SUV. He was right, of course. We didn't have to have a beach wedding. It was just something that crossed my mind last summer. Now I wished we had done it then when my son Thad and his fiancée, Sarah, were visiting. My daughter Jennifer and her new boyfriend Dylan lived close enough that they could drive over anytime we decided to get married. But it was a little harder for Thad and Sarah. I picked up a big box that was filled with bathroom items from the back of the SUV, and Alec was right behind me.

"You're just avoiding the question, aren't you?"

I shook my head and headed toward the house with my box. I was getting soaked from the rain and wished we had chosen a better time to unload the boxes. "I'm not avoiding the subject. I'm thinking."

I hurried into the house, but it was no use. I was soaked.

Alec hurried with two more boxes behind me. "Well, what are you thinking? Can't you think out loud so I know what's going through that beautiful red head of yours?"

I shook my head and laughed. "No, I can't think out loud. But I'm thinking about the wedding. We don't need anything fancy, but what about my mom? And my brother and sister? They're going to have to travel from Alabama."

"Okay, then set a date, and they can travel. Why is this so difficult?"

I set my box down with the others.

"It's not hard. I just don't know what I want to do."

He set his boxes down, glanced around the ballroom, and turned to me. "Why don't we do it here?"

I stopped. "Here?" I glanced around the room. It was lovely. We could rent some chairs and do the wedding and the reception here. It was a great idea. I smiled at him. "All right, then. Let's do it here."

He nodded and grinned. "It's a plan then. When?"

I stopped. "I'll have to check with Sarah, and my mom, and Jake and Shelby."

He narrowed his eyes at me. "You're trying to put me off again, aren't you?"

I shook my head. "No, of course not. But if there's any chance they can all make it here, then I want to pick a date that they can come."

"Why don't you just pick a date and tell him that's what it is. You know they're going to do everything they can to get here.

And then if for some reason somebody genuinely can't make it on that date, we could set it back a week."

He had a point. "Okay then. Next month."

He shook his head. "Next weekend."

I stared at him. "Next weekend? You're out of your mind. How about two weeks from now?" It was out of my mouth before I had time to think about it. Two weeks? Could I put a wedding together in two weeks?

He nodded. "Deal. We're getting married in two weeks."

I opened my mouth. "Oh, wait a minute, that's too soon. We can't do it in two weeks."

He laughed. "You know what? We're going to do it in two weeks."

And that was how I got roped in to getting married without enough time to prepare for my wedding.

Printed in Great Britain
by Amazon